I WANTED A PONY

I WANTED A PONY

DIANA PULLEIN-THOMPSON

Armada

First published in the U.K. by
William Collins Sons & Co. Ltd., London and Glasgow.
This edition was first published in 1966 by
May Fair Books Ltd., 14 St. James's Place,
London S.W.1.

© Diana Pullein-Thompson 1966

Printed by Love & Malcomson Ltd.,
Brighton Road, Redhill, Surrey.

CONTENTS

CHAPTER ONE

I CAN remember very well the first few weeks of my long stay at Tree Tops. For me they were rather dull, although not uneventful, weeks. My cousins, who each have a pony of their own, went out riding every day except Sundays and I, who couldn't ride well enough to manage their ponies, stayed behind, which was dull because, except for reading, there was nothing nice to do.

In those days I disliked my cousins more than I do now because they seemed to despise me; they were very scornful about anything they did not agree with and they often told me that *honestly* I was *queer*. They were amazed and slightly contemptuous, too, when they found that I did not know what horsey phrases like "behind the bit" and "herring gutted" meant. Actually, I believe that *they* often brought them into their conversation, so as to impress people. Jill used to swank a lot; during the first week I was at Tree Tops she frequently talked about the prizes she and her show pony, Sunshine, had won and the compliments they had been paid by the leading judges. I was even more idiotic then than I am now and because I had never won anything, those stories used to make me feel very small and stupid.

I had only ridden a little on a fat, piebald, half-shetland pony called Dominoe. He belonged to Penny Davis, a girl of eight, who lived in a house quite near the cottage in which Mummy and I lived. Dominoe spent most of the spring and autumn in our orchard and Penny and I often rode him bareback before breakfast. We also practised what we called circus tricks—we taught him to shake hands and stand on a tub, and ourselves to canter facing the tail. Of course we were always falling off and sometimes Dominoe got sick of us—then he used to kick.

One day, several weeks before my parents went abroad and I went to live at Tree Tops, I rode Dominoe in a little Pony Club Gymkhana, which, by a cruel stroke of fate, my cousins were watching. I competed in the best rider class and the bending race under fourteen years. In the riding class Dominoe bucked; I fell off and was the first person to be called in to start a back line, which was made out of the worst riders in the class. In the bending race Dominoe took charge and calmly and firmly carried me out of the ring, much to the amusement of the spectators. I don't think I am frightfully self-conscious, but I must say I felt awful about being taken out of the ring; I knew that I had been terribly feeble and I expect you can imagine my horror when I found that my cousins had seen everything. Of course, they were very scornful.

Barbara, who is the eldest and fourteen, said, "Oh! *really*, Augusta, you *did* look funny." Stephen said that even the soppiest chap at his school could have stuck on Dominoe in the riding class, and that I wasn't holding my reins properly. Jill said that Dominoe was an awful pony and much too fat, and that I should have used a "diagonal aid" when he started to "play up."

I was furious. I felt my face getting red and a knot in my throat and for an awful moment I thought I was going to cry, but I didn't; I swallowed hard and then, in almost my usual voice, I said that Dominoe was not awful, but very intelligent, and that I should like to see one of them controlling him. This was a very silly remark, and I instantly regretted making it, because I knew that it was my bad riding which had made Dominoe "play up," as Jill put it, and anyway, my cousins knew much more about ponies and were far better riders than me.

Jill stared at me in amazement, and then she said, "Gosh! You *are* conceited."

Stephen said, "How much do you bet I can't control him?"

I said that I must ask Penny whether he could ride Dominoe, and I was just setting off in search of her, when she appeared and asked what we were saying about her.

Stephen said, "Can I ride Dominoe?"

Penny didn't notice the face I made, which meant say no, and, being not at all a selfish person, she said, "Yes, certainly, if you're not too heavy."

"Of course he's not," said Jill. "A Shetland pony is a miniature carthorse and, like a carthorse, is not suitable for riding, but very strong."

I remember noticing that she spoke as though she knew the sentence off by heart.

Stephen mounted without saying thank you, and made Dominoe canter in a sort of circle; then he rode round outside the ring and, as I expect you have guessed, he managed to control him easily. When he dismounted, he said, "My, he's nappy."

"He must be awful to ride," said Jill. "He's so terribly broad, and he's got no front at all."

"Yes, he's certainly jolly rough and this blinking little saddle keeps on slipping forwards—he ought to have a crupper," said Stephen, looking scornfully at Penny's third-hand saddle.

9

"He's not awful," I said. "And, if he *is* like a cart-horse or all wrong in shape, that's not his fault. You aren't so very good looking yourselves."

"Talk away, baby," said Stephen.

"She thinks she knows so much that she doesn't need to learn anything from more experienced riders," said Barbara in a calm and despising voice.

"I certainly don't want to learn anything from you. I don't like your riding, and I hate you," I said furiously.

At that moment the collecting ring steward announced the first entry in the children's jumping, and Jill said, "Come on, let's leave the conceited little baby."

They went away and I set off in search of Penny, who had miraculously disappeared, and Mummy. I found them and Mummy *would* go and talk to my cousins, because she hadn't seen them for a long time, and I had great difficulty in avoiding them. I spent the rest of the afternoon thinking of all the dignified and cutting retorts I might have made to their contemptuous remarks.

After the gymkhana Penny, who, by the way, didn't enter because her parents decided that she was too young, and I made a determined effort to improve our riding. We gave up the circus tricks and we rode with pennies under our knees to make us keep them close to the saddle, and mostly in a saddle and bridle. I think we had improved quite a lot when I went to Tree Tops; anyway, we could keep our toes up and hold the reins properly.

I remember that, during the first two days I was at Tree Tops, I thought my cousins would never forget the gymkhana; they were exasperating. When I remarked to Stephen that his pony, Sandy, had a nice intelligent head, he hooted with laughter and said, sarcastically, that he was sure that he couldn't be nearly so intelligent as Dominoe, because he hadn't learned how to avoid bending races yet. When I asked if I might have a tiny ride on Barbara's pony, Sweep, she told me that he had been carefully schooled by an expert and that she didn't want me to spoil him and teach him to take charge of people. When I asked any of them questions about schooling ponies, they said that they thought I hated them and didn't want to learn from them. Luckily it soon wore off, although they never offered me a ride on their ponies.

Another thing, which made Tree Tops dull for me at the beginning of my stay, was not having any animals of my own, for although my parents were poor I had always had a few animals and it seemed odd to have nothing to look after. At the start of the Easter holidays I had two white Aylesbury ducks, called Dilly and Dally. They had bright-yellow beaks and they were very clever. I wanted to take them to Tree Tops, but Aunt Margaret said that they would get into the garden and eat the greens. I suggested that I might keep them in a run in the ponies' field, but she said that Sunshine, being a highly-bred pony, was very nervous and might get tangled up in the wire netting and blemish herself—then she wouldn't win any more showing classes.

That is typical of Aunt Margaret, and I'm sure that as long as her children and their ponies went on winning, she wouldn't mind if they caused all the ducks in the world to be destroyed. Actually, I gave Dilly and Dally to Penny, and I expect they were very happy, because I have since found out that ducks, although clever, are not affectionate.

I also had, at that time, an enormous tortoise, called

11

Matilda, which I did take to Tree Tops, with fatal results. Two days after I arrived I let her out on the lawn and sat down and started to read one of Jill's books on horsemanship; it was very interesting and I was horrible enough to forget all about poor Matilda, who must have crawled slowly off the lawn. Somehow she got into the field, where my cousins were schooling their ponies, and Barbara, who did not know she was there, rode Sweep on top of her and killed her. Barbara said that she would buy me a new tortoise. I sniffed, and said that no tortoise could ever replace Matilda."

Stephen said, "Fancy crying over a silly old tortoise," and Aunt Margaret said that I had only myself to blame. I told Stephen to shut up, and I made up my mind that if I have any children and if they, by mistake, help to cause one of their animals' death, however angry I feel I won't tell them that they have only themselves to blame. It is horrible to feel that an animal has been killed through your carelessness, and I still feel miserable when I think about poor Matilda.

After her death I found it rather difficult to think of things to do while my cousins were riding, although it was all right when they were schooling in the field, because I used to watch them. My aunt's house is not at all interesting; it is neither big nor small nor old nor modern—it is just middling. I don't like the garden much either; it is very little good for hide-and-seek or murders, because it is full of lily ponds and rock-gardens, and there is an awful row if you fall into the lily ponds or put a foot on the rock-gardens. There are no screens or bushes to hide behind for hide-and-seek, but there are a few young fir-trees either side of the drive, which, unfortunately, are no good for climbing. The whole place is too tidy—at least, I think so—and I was always getting into rows for not wiping my feet and for not putting things back in their places. Aunt Margaret often told me that she wasn't going to have mud spread about *her* house *or* have me make it like a pigsty. "You're not at Blenheim Cottage now," she would invariably finish up.

Blenheim Cottage is the name of the low, tiled roofed, cream-washed cottage in which Mummy and I lived, while Daddy spent the week days in London and joined us at the week-ends. Aunt Margaret is Daddy's sister, and I think she disapproved of Mummy. She is certain that our cottage was always like a pigsty, because she once paid us a surprise visit and found the parlour in an awful mess. Mummy and I were searching for a pair of scissors—I've forgotten what we wanted them for—and we had turned out all the drawers and cupboards in the room and we hadn't put anything back, so you can imagine what the floor looked like. Aunt Margaret is rather proper and she was very shocked. Then things were made worse, because she went into the kitchen, through the dining-room door, at the same moment as Nightmare and her six chicks, Nigel, Nellie, Nicholas, Nancy, Neptune and Nero, came in through the back door. They looked very sweet and Mummy and I were both overcome by violent giggles. Aunt Margaret was dumbfounded and since that day she has been convinced that we purposely taught our hens to come into the kitchen. Actually, that was the first time that any of them had come into the house, and I suppose it was just fate that Nightmare should make her entry at the same moment as Aunt Margaret. I think my cousins were told about Nightmare and that is one of the reasons that they think I'm "queer."

Barbara and Stephen were often told off for being untidy, too, but Jill rarely was; partly, I think, be-

13

cause she is a tidier character and partly because she is Aunt Margaret's favourite.

During my third week at Tree Tops my cousins competed in a horse show and gymkhana, but before I tell you about it I think I had better tell you a little about their ponies. Sweep is black and 14.1 hands high and is good looking, except for his head which is rather coarse. He seems to be permanently in a bad temper, and he doesn't carry himself so well as Sunshine. He was a trained jumper when Aunt Margaret bought him, and he always strikes me as being sick to death of gymkhanas, but Barbara says he loves them. Sunshine is chestnut, with four white socks and very showy. She has a beautiful temper and has been carefully schooled by an expert. Jill told me the other day that she had cost 150 guineas. Stephen's pony, Sandy, is in many ways the nicest of the three, although he is the least schooled. He is much better-natured than Sweep and not so nervous as Sunshine, and his colour —a golden-dun—is unusual. He pulls and tears about, but he seems definitely to enjoy jumping, and I should think he's a marvellous hunter.

The ponies are looked after by a man called Curtis, who drives the car as well. They live in the stable practically all the year round, because in the winter they are clipped for hunting and in the spring and summer they are going in for horse shows, and my cousins say that they couldn't possibly ride ponies which are blown out with grass.

The ponies were smartly plaited for the horse show, which was a very posh affair with expensive cups, presented by rich and well-known people, and they travelled over in a frightfully smart horse-box. Curtis went with them, and the rest of us by car. I couldn't help thinking that if I was one of my cousins I would

Both were silver and very large.

much rather go in the horse-box and see what the ponies thought of the journey.

The first event, in which Jill and Sunshine were competing, was a showing class for ponies under fourteen-two hands; there was a large entry, and to my inexperienced eyes, all the ponies looked beautifully made and very superior, but Aunt Margaret found lots wrong with them. The judges spent a long time making up their minds, which annoyed Barbara and Stephen, who said that any fool could see that Sunshine was miles better than the other ponies. At last Jill was given a red rosette and then, much to Aunt Margaaret's joy, she was handed two cups by Lord Langley, who looked very self-conscious and was unsuitably dressed in town clothes. One cup was the first prize for the best pony and the other was a special prize for the best rider in the class; both were silver and very large, and I thought slightly ugly. When Jill came out of the ring a press photographer took a photograph of her on Sunshine with one in each hand. I am sure that I would have scowled if it had been me, but she put on a sporting smile and I may as well tell you now that the photograph came out beautifully and that Aunt Margaret showed it with pride to all her friends, in spite of the fact that most of them told her that they had already seen it in the local paper.

All my cousins were in the next event, which was a children's jumping class. Barbara won first after jumping two clear rounds on Sweep. Stephen and Sandy were third—they refused once at the wall, which was red and white, and very solid. Jill and Sunshine were completely out of it because they refused the gate, which was away from the entrance, twice, and knocked down the triple bars. Barbara was awarded a cup, but this time the presenter, who handed it to her, was not a lord.

After the jumping there was a hack class and after that we had lunch. Then there was a class for heavy-weight hunters, which was followed by bending and potato races and musical chairs, which were exciting to watch, but which reminded me of my disgraceful performance on Dominoe. Stephen won all three of these, and Barbara and Jill each won a second. Stephen said that he had done pretty well even for him, and Jill said that it wasn't fair—one of her potatoes had bounced out of the bucket and had been counted as a miss, and the music had been deliberately stopped whenever she was behind a jump. Barbara told her that she was a bad loser, and Aunt Margaret said that

Jill was quite right and people were going out of their way to stop her winning, because they were jealous of her being such a good rider. At this moment I managed to slip off on my own and watch the remaining events by myself, which was much nicer than sitting in the stuffy car looking proper, as Aunt Margaret had insisted on me doing the whole afternoon.

The Open Jumping was the last event.

The Open Jumping was the last event, and I enjoyed watching it the most, although some of the riders seemed to knock their horses about rather a lot. It was won by a man on a chestnut cob with very high action; they were the only competitors to jump a clear round, and I thought they jumped very nicely, but afterwards Jill told me that the cob had no scope and that he would have been flummoxed if there had been a water jump. While the competitors were being called into the ring to get their rosettes, Aunt Margaret fetched me; she was a little angry and said that I *was* a queer girl—standing amongst the crowd with the sun in my eyes, when I could be sitting in the car for which she had paid five shillings to park at the ringside. I didn't tell her that the car was stuffy or that I couldn't bear her constant criticisms of all the ponies and children, except her own, a moment longer; instead I lied and said that I had wanted to get a closer glimpse of the wall. She said that it didn't take two hours to look at a wall and we walked to the car in disagreeable silence.

On the way home, Jill grumbled about Sunshine's jumping; at first she said it was Curtis's fault that she hadn't won, because he couldn't have given her enough oats. Then, on second thoughts, she said that she supposed it was rather a lot to expect a show pony to be a jumper as well, and that what she needed was a trained show jumper of 14.1 hands high—then she would win everywhere.

To my surprise Aunt Margaret didn't tell her to shut up and stop grumbling; instead she said, "Well, dear, is there anything to stop you having one? I'm willing to pay for it and, of course, we can just keep Sunshine for the showing classes; that's what I bought her for."

"Oh, Mummy!" said Jill. "Do you really mean it? Gosh! I shall win everywhere."

"I know, dear," said Aunt Margaret quietly.

"It isn't fair," said Stephen. "Can't I have one too? Jill always has everything."

"I don't," said Jill.

"You do," said Stephen.

"*Children*, stop quarrelling at once. I can only buy one jumper, and as Jill is the best rider she must have it," said Aunt Margaret sharply.

"It's not cricket," said Stephen. "Just because Jill wins best-rider prizes doesn't mean she's the best of us at jumping. I beat her to-day, so why shouldn't I have the jumper?"

"Look here, Stephen," said Aunt Margaret, "if you are going to argue and grumble I'm going to sell Sandy and have done with it. Everybody knows that Jill is the best rider—Lord Stanwell said so himself, and he ought to know."

"Beastly liar," muttered Stephen.

I am sure that if I had been Jill I should have felt very mean at being so obviously favoured, but she seemed pleased; she actually smiled and then she said that she would soon be beating Susan Phillips and John Dunlop hollow. In case you don't know, I think I had better tell you that they are both professional show jumping children, who win hundreds of prizes a year.

Barbara did not seem to be at all annoyed that Jill was so favoured; she laughed and said that the professionals needed waking up and Jill laughed too, and said that she would do more than wake them up—she would beat them every time they dared to show their faces in a ring. Aunt Margaret smiled and said, "Your name will be in every paper, darling."

This conversation made me feel slightly sick, but I said nothing and, although Aunt Margaret drove slowly, we were soon back at Tree Tops. It was half-past seven and, after we had eaten dinner, and pulled all the ponies at the show, except my cousins', methodically to pieces, Aunt Margaret and Jill wrote an advertisement for *Horse and Hound*.

19

It was this:

Absolutely first-class jumper of about 14.1 h.h., must have cleared five foot. Good price paid for right animal. Apply, Miss J. Fielding, Tree Tops, Fledgewood, Flintshire.

They read it out aloud and I remember thinking how boastful it sounded; then suddenly I wished that my parents would buy me a simply marvellous pony, so that I could beat that super child rider, Jill Fielding, at every show in the country—no, more, at every show where she "dared to show her face." I smiled as I thought how angry she would be at being thwarted by a "queer" person like me. I could see her trying to make up excuses—probably she would blame Curtis.

Of course, it was a silly wish, because there are lots more important things in the world than winning, and most likely I would have instantly become horrible and have only thought of my pony as a means to being admired and getting my name in the papers.

CHAPTER TWO

THE two days following the show were beastly. My cousins grumbled and quarrelled nearly the whole time. Stephen was still furious that Jill was going to have two ponies and Barbara was cross because Sweep had bitten her arm and left a big blue bruise. Everything was made worse by the weather, which was frightful; it rained and rained, and I kept forgetting to wipe my feet, which was a constant source of unpleasantness. Aunt Margaret wouldn't let us go out of doors much because of getting chills and there was nothing to do indoors except play table tennis or read. My cousins don't like reading, and they were always asking me to make a fourth for the tennis. I hated this because I was a much worse player than they, and whenever one of them was unlucky enough to draw me as a partner, he or she groaned and then sighed and made despairing grimaces, when I missed the ball or hit it off the board, both of which sins I committed far more often than my cousins, who seemed experts. If Aunt Margaret happened to be watching, she would tell my partner to remember that not every one was so good at games as him or herself, and then sometimes she would tell them not to grumble because it wasn't my fault that I was so *hopeless* at games.

My stupidity and these remarks exasperated me and when, during a game in the evening of the second day, I feebly missed the ball for the third time running and Jill, my partner, made a peculiarly irritating grimace, I threw my bat at her. For once my aim was true, the bat hit her on the nose and to my surprise she burst into tears. Stephen said that she was a cry-baby and Barbara that she must be quiet or Aunt Margaret would hear, but Jill obstinately screamed, "My nose; oh, my nose." Of course Aunt Margaret *did* hear, and I got into an awful row and was sent to bed without any supper, which I didn't mind terribly because, having spent all day indoors, I wasn't hungry. I turned on the light by my bed when it got dark, and read until ten o'clock, when Aunt Margaret found me. She was very angry and gave me a long lecture on disobedience, which, since she had never told me not to read, was rather out of place—at least that's what I thought at the time.

Next morning dawned fair and every one seemed in better tempers, although Jill complained that her nose ached. At breakfast my cousins decided to go for a long ride and take sandwiches for lunch. Aunt Margaret suggested that I should go with them on Jill's bicycle, but Jill made a face and said that it had a slow puncture in the back tyre. Because I did not want to go for a long ride on a bike with my quarrelling cousins, I quickly suggested that I should go for a long picnic walk on my own and explore the countryside. At first Aunt Margaret was against my idea; she said that I might get lost and that I wouldn't be very safe alone. But I pointed out that I was nearly twelve and that, being an only child, I was used to doing things by myself, also that I could take a map and ask the way. My cousins, who obviously did not want me to go with them, backed me up with most convincing arguments and after a bit she said that I could go.

Barbara made a rough map of the way to Bi End Common, which I had decided to explore, and at eleven o'clock when my cousins rode away down the drive, I set out across the tranquil green meadows, which lie behind Tree Tops, with a light heart, although I little knew what fate held in store for me.

It was a beautiful morning, with perfect walking weather; the sun shone with all the sparkling brilliance of late April, while idle clouds floated in the pale-blue sky, chivied by a gentle breeze. I walked slowly, now and again looking at my map, and trying to invent poetry about the fields around me. I was not very successful, and I couldn't think of any rhymes, so I gave up and fell to deciding what I would do if I was given

22

a thousand pounds. I arranged that I would buy a small farmhouse with a white front door and about ten acres, and that I would have two ponies and a brood mare and a black spaniel, with flopping ears. Then I began to feel more energetic and pretended to be a beautiful grey Anglo-Arab, called Marsala. I cantered and bucked, and refused a fallen tree twice, and vaulted over a gate. But I soon got puffed and, not being really an energetic person, I broke into a walk again. A church clock struck one and I decided to have lunch; I sat down on some grass by the side of a ploughed field and ate the ham sandwiches Mrs. Smith, the cook, had kindly made me. I felt glad that Aunt Margaret was not there to tell me not to sit on the damp grass, and I wondered whether my cousins had eaten their lunch.

When I had finished I thought I would look at Barbara's map and make sure that I was going the right way, but I found that it had gone, and then I realised that it had probably fallen out of my pocket, while I was pretending to be Marsala. I wasn't sure which was the right way, so I tried to see the map in my mind's eye. After a bit I remembered Barbara telling me that Big End Common had a church, and I decided to go in what I thought was the direction of the church clock that had struck one. I headed right and took a track by the side of a wheat field. I walked for what seemed like ages, and the countryside became more hilly and the fields smaller, but I saw no sign of a church. I began to think that I might be walking in a circle and to wonder whether I had been walking for a long time, and then to my joy, I saw smoke rising from a dip in the hills ahead. Thinking that it came from a farmhouse or cottage, I hurried on. I walked up a long slope and looked down into the valley. To

23

my horror I saw that it was not the slow curling smoke that comes from a farmhouse chimney, but smoke rising in hurried, angry clouds from blazing ricks. I stood gazing in amazement for a few seconds and then I simply tore down the hill, but when I reached the fire I was rooted to the spot. I could see that something ought to be done as quickly as possible —fire engines were needed—but I couldn't decide what would be the quickest way to summon them; there was no house in sight and no road that I could see; and I remember that I cursed myself for being a fool, because I felt sure that if my cousins had been there they would not have stood like me, in a frenzy of indecision while the fire blazed, unchecked. They would have found some way to get the fire engines, and they would not have wasted time when every moment counted But I didn't stay gazing at the flames (some of which were darting along the ground, catching stray wisps of hay and straw and drawing nearer, every moment, to a barn with a hole in the roof), for very long. I walked through a gate to the left of the fire, which led into an almost square farmyard. I had hoped to see some sign of life, but as I looked round my heart sank. The place was deserted; the doors of the long, low buildings, which made three sides of the yard and which might have been stables or cows' stalls, were shut and locked, and weeds, which were growing rampant in the gateway, told plainly that few hoofs had passed through that way of late. There were pigsties too, with ragged roofs and nettles mocking in their unused runs, but I did not look at *them* for long, because to my joy I noticed that behind them was a cottage. I ran across to it and was at once disappointed, for the back door was locked, and the cottage also showed no sign of life. It did not seem likely that it would be on the telephone, but I ran round to the front and found that there was a narrow stony lane leading to the cottage and that in the lane were telephone wires. All seemed easy then, and I ran to what was obviously the front door, and tried to open it, but it was locked; I banged it twice and then I looked through a window, and my heart leapt because I saw a telephone sitting right in front of me on the window ledge. Of course the window was firmly latched, but I seized a stone and broke a hole in a pane. I put my hand through and undid the latch, and opened it. Then I picked up the receiver and after what seemed like ages, a voice said, "Number, please?"

"Fire station, please," I said.

"Hold the line," said the operator.

Then after what again seemed like ages, a man's voice said:

"Dilford Fire Station."

I said, "Please send a fire engine quickly, there are some ricks on fire here, and all the farm buildings will be alight in a minute."

The voice said, "Where are you speaking from?"

These words tied my tongue for a moment and then I idiotically said, "I don't know, it's no good, I don't know."

"Pardon?" said the voice.

"I don't know," I shouted. "I'm somewhere near a church clock and not far from Big End Common." I added on second thoughts.

"Look here," said the voice. "If you are trying to be funny I may as well tell you now that you're trying the wrong person."

"Don't be stupid," I said. "I'm not trying to be funny. I haven't got quite such a silly sense of humour. I am out for a picnic walk and I have come upon this

25

The roof was blazing gaily.

farm, which is in a valley and has a lane leading to it, and unless you come quickly the whole place will be burnt."

"Well, perhaps if you could explain the whereabouts of the farm you mention, a little plainer, I might be able to help you," said the voice in maddeningly calm tones.

I said, "Well, I'll tell you all I know—it is a pretty big farm, surrounded by fields with oats and wheat in them, and all the stable doors are locked, and the yard is large and square, and the roofs of the buildings have holes, but," I said, looking round me, "the cottage I am in has no cobwebs to speak of, and must have been used quite lately, though there's no furniture."

"All right, miss. I know the place. We'll come along right away," the voice interrupted, sounding suddenly agreeable. Then it rang off.

I put the receiver down and suddenly I realised that probably the telephone number was on the telephone, and that it might have helped enormously if I had known what exchange I was on. I cursed myself for being a fool and then I looked, and I must say I was relieved when I saw that, if there ever had been a disc, it had gone.

I whistled and slammed the window and tore off to see how the fire was. I found that it had spread more quickly than I would have imagined possible. Two ricks were completely burned and the barn with a hole in the roof was blazing gaily; a third rick in front of a Dutch barn, filled with unthrashed oats, was threatened by flames dashing along the straw-strewn ground. I couldn't stand and watch and do nothing, so I ran off in search of a hose or bucket; I found neither, but I came across an old shovel lying in one of the broken-down pigsties; I seized it and simply tore back to the scene of disaster. Once there, I started to beat out the flames, which were approaching the Dutch barn and rick. It was terribly hot work and the smoke made me cough until I thought my lungs would burst, and my eyes watered. Now and then parts of the blazing barn collapsed with a sickening crash, and then sparks flew in all directions, making the fire still larger. My beating seemed to do little good and I was hampered by having to stop every few minutes to wipe my eyes and cough. I began to wonder whether the fire engines were ever going to come; peraps they thought I meant quite a different farm; they might be miles away by now, for all I knew.

Suddenly my dismal thoughts were interrupted by a footstep, and then a voice said, "It 'baint no use you doing that, miss. What you wants is one of them fire engines from Dilford. Why, *all* them buildings will be alight in a minute, and then I don't know what the captain will say, that I don't."

The voice belonged to an old man, who looked as though he might be a farm labourer. For a moment I felt like being rude but I wasn't. I put down my shovel and told him that the fire engines were already on their way. "Actually," I added, "they should be here any moment now."

He seemed surprised, and he said, "Lor' lumme," several times. Then I asked him why the farm was so deserted and he said that it was a long story, and that it was what came of employing Irishmen. I was filled with curiosity and, while I started to beat at the flames in a half-hearted manner, I asked what Irishmen had to do with the fate of the farm. He said again that it was a long story, and then he explained that when he was a boy the place had belonged to Lord Thorley, who lived in Dewey Park, nearly two miles away. The farm had looked a treat then; the stables had been full of valuable bloodstock, the yard speckless and the hedges, parting the green fields, had been clipped twice a year—spring and autumn. So well arranged was everything that no man employed by Lord Thorley ever had cause to complain. Then suddenly he died, at the age of seventy—although you would never have guessed it—and the place was never the same again. His son took no interest in farming or horses; he was more interested in racing cars than anything else, and he wouldn't put any money into keeping the place up. Most of the men left and those that stayed took no pride in their work. The hedges grew high and ragged; tiles, that fell from the roofs of the buildings, were not replaced; the yard, once so speckless, became a vast manure heap, and weeds flourished where once grew green pasture.

Ten years after Lord Thorley's death you wouldn't have known it for the same place, so changed had it become. Then tragedy overtook the son and he was killed in a car crash, like every one had foretold. The place was sold to a jumped-up Londoner, who fancied that he knew something about farming and decided to turn it into arable land. He ordered the hedges to be destroyed, so that they would not shelter the crops from the sun, and where he needed fences he put up wire. He lived in a house on the common, and he had the cottage at the farm done up, and put on the telephone, and let it to some of his London friends.

All went fairly well until he developed a fell complaint—the old man could not remember the name. Then he went abroad for treatment, leaving the farm in charge of an Irishman, who let the place go to rack and ruin, cooked the accounts and finally made off with a lot of money. That was three months before the day of the fire and seven weeks later the disheartened Londoner, who was still languishing in foreign lands in search of a specialist, who could cure him, sold the farm to a Captain Houseman for next to nothing, complete with last year's ricks and oats. Owing to shortage of labour and Captain Houseman being busy on his other farm, nothing yet had been done to the place, but the people living in the cottage had moved out a month after it was sold, and he hoped to put a working foreman in there as soon as possible, so luckily, he had not had it cut off the telephone.

As the old man finished his depressing story I heard, to my joy, the urgent sound of fire engines' bells. It drew nearer and nearer, gay and assuring, ringing in my ears and chasing away all misgivings from my mind, as the breeze had chased the threatening clouds from the sky that morning.

"Hurray," I shouted, "they're coming!" And I chucked my shovel in the air and caught it. Then I had a fit of coughing and by the time I had finished the fire engines had arrived. There were two of them and they were bright, red and shiny. The firemen lost no time; in a few minutes they had found the water main, and were pouring water through their thick hoses on to the blazing barn.

It is surprising how quickly news spreads and crowds collect. Very soon after the fire engines had arrived, a mass of people had assembled, whether because they had heard the bells or seen the red glow in the sky, I do not know. Some of them found pieces of brushwood and planks, and they helped to beat out the flames—they seemed much more effective than I had been. The old man, who appeared to be an unhelpful sort of person, amused himself by telling any

30

one he could capture, how and when he came across the fire, and what he would have done had he been me. Gradually the flames grew fewer and paler, although the barn was beyond saving.

Then a car came down the stony lane and drew to a standstill by the cottage. Several people said, "Here's the Captain." And a tall man in corduroy trousers got out, followed by two black spaniels. He talked to some of the firemen and to the old man, and then, to my surprise, he came to me. He said that he wanted to thank me for calling in the fire brigade; but for my swift action, he said, he might have been a ruined man. I said that I had done nothing—it had only been a matter of ringing up. He said, that from what he heard, he should say that it was a matter of courage, and that he understood that I had stopped the fire from spreading to the Dutch barn and rick with an old shovel. The rick alone, he said was worth nearly two hundred pounds and the oats were worth more. Then he asked me my name and address, and added that he hoped to make me a small present, in return for saving his farm, later on. I said again that I had done nothing and that it was only luck that I had come across the farm. Then I said that as all the excitement was over and it was getting late, I thought I had better be starting for home; and he thanked me again as I left.

The walk back was lovely; a brisk spring shower made my hair wet and rain water ran down my face in warm trickles, making pale, twisting channels in the black dirt that covered it. I whistled gay tunes like "The Isle of Capri" and recited poetry about stirring deeds like "Horatius," and I was glad that my cousins were not there to tell me that I was "queer." Annoying fits of coughing occasionally interrupted me, but luckily they did not last for long and, although I still

31

had a faint taste of smoke in my mouth, when I reached Tree Tops, I had completely overcome my coughing.

I passed the dining-room window on my way to the front door and, looking in, I saw that my cousins were at tea. They were eating bread and honey, all fair-haired, clean and tidy; they looked very respectable and very English. I wondered what they would say when I walked in and told them about the fire. Barbara would probably smile, slowly and superiorly. Jill would wrinkle her ugly snub nose, as she always did when she disapproved of or disbelieved anything. Stephen would probably say, "Tell us another." I decided it was fun standing and looking at them, rather like watching films, before they became talkies, must have been, I thought. But soon the sight of bread and honey made me feel hungry, and I went indoors. I washed my hands and face, because I knew that if I didn't I would only be made to before I was allowed any tea. Then, whistling gaily, I ran downstairs into the dining-room.

Aunt Margaret had just come in—obviously some one had rung up in answer to the advertisement in *Horse and Hound*. "It sounds just the thing, dear," she was saying; "it's a snowy grey of fourteen one and it's cleared five foot. She says it's very keen and not at all suitable for a beginner, but I said that, as you're such an experienced rider, that was all to the good. . . . Oh, hullo, Augusta, you have been out a long time," she exclaimed, seeing me.

"I'm afraid I'm late," I said.

"When can we see it, Mummy?" asked Jill.

"I thought you wouldn't want to wait, so I arranged for us to go over and try it to-morrow afternoon. It's at Steadly Green, near Fieldbank which is about twenty miles the other side of Dilford. By the way, it's a gelding and it's won nineteen firsts out of the twenty-two jumping classes it competed in last year," said Aunt Margaret.

"You will be able to jump him at Olympia, and Richmond, and Islington," said Barbara.

"Perhaps Dublin later on," added Aunt Margaret.

When I had come into the room I had been in a good temper, but now I felt crosser and crosser, the more they talked about the pony. I am afraid that I was jealous and I couldn't help wishing that it was I who was going to jump at Olympia on a grey gelding. So when Barbara politely asked me whether I had had a nice walk and managed to find my way to Big End Common successfully, I only angrily muttered that I had had a nice walk, thank you.

"My, you sound in a bait," said Stephen. "What's the matter, Gussy? Did you lose your way or meet a gamekeeper?"

"No, I didn't meet a gamekeeper, thank you," I said, and I expect I scowled.

"Mummy," said Jill, "what's his name and what shows did he win at?"

"Goodness knows, but we'll find that out tomorrow, my pet," said Aunt Margaret.

Then, as every one had finished eating, my cousins went away and tinkered with the wireless. I fetched a book and read until dinner-time.

At dinner Jill started to talk about the grey, and the tests she would give him when she tried him the next day. Aunt Margaret went on to explain how famous Jill would become when she won the jumping at Olympia. The fire at the farm began to seen so small an incident, compared with their far-reaching plans, that by the time we were eating the second course, I had decided not to mention it. I expect you think that I was silly, but actually I have never regretted it.

CHAPTER THREE

THE next day was Sunday. Aunt Margaret said that we must go to church, which was very awkward for me, because I had no hat other than an old straw one, which Mummy had bought for me to wear in the garden on hot summer days; it had cost sixpence and had come from Woolworth's, but it was plain with no horrible flowers on the front, and I liked it. Of course, it was not at all suitable for going to church, and Aunt Margaret made me try on all my cousin's many, smug hats. They were much too small and, perched on top of my head, they made me look ridiculous. I could not stop giggling and after a bit Aunt Margaret got fed up and asked what happened when I went to church at home. I had to admit that I didn't go at all often and that the last time I had gone had been in the summer, and I had worn my straw hat.

"Not that shabby thing," said Aunt Margaret incredulously.

"You must have looked queer," said Barbara.

"What do you wear when it rains?" asked Jill.

"Nothing, of course," I replied.

Aunt Margaret said that it was a wonder I hadn't got pneumonia, and I said that I hoped I wasn't quite such a weakling that I couldn't get my hair wet without being ill. This remark annoyed her and she started to lecture on the badness of my character. Luckily, she had only got as far as telling me that I was ridiculous and rude, when Barbara suggested that I should go to church with a handkerchief tied over my head.

Jill said that I should look "queer," but Aunt Margaret said that, since I appeared to have no hat of my own, she supposed that it was the only thing to do, although I would look an awful fright. I said that I didn't mind looking a fright, and I borrowed a large blue handkerchief from Barbara.

After church, Stephen said that I had started several people giggling by my funny appearance. It was a good thing that I wasn't in my straw hat, looking like a farmer's boy, he said, or goodness knew what might have happened. I said that I was glad that I had given some one a little amusement, and that anyway, he should listen to the sermon when he was at church, not to giggling people. He said that it wasn't during the sermon, but in the middle of a hymn. "So there!" he added triumphantly. I said that it made no difference, he should have been attending to the hymn. He said that I was a prig and I said that I wasn't, and he said that I was one of the most babyish and conceited girls he had ever met, and I said that he was beneath contempt. Then, luckily, Aunt Margaret heard and said that unless we stopped quarrelling immediately we would both be sent straight to bed; so the silly argument ended.

After lunch we all started for Steadley Green, to see the pony, in the car. On the way over we tried to imagine what he would be like. I said that he would be a dock-tailed cob with a wise head and a keen temperament, and that he would be called Cocky, and would pull Jill's arms out. Stephen said that he would be an eighteen-year-old windsucker with a mass of splints and spavins and an uncertain temper. Barbara said that he would be an extremely beautiful, part-

35

bred Arab with a flowing mane and tail, called Moon-stone; and Jill said that we were all wrong, because she was certain that he would be perfect in every way and a really super jumper.

Eventually we reached Steadley Green and found the house. Aunt Margaret knocked at the front door, which was opened by the owner of the pony, Mrs. Payne. She was a hard-faced woman in a hair net, and she said that she had been expecting us, and that the pony was in the stable.

"He's an absolute topper," she said, "and he can jump as high as his ears."

"At which shows has he won?" asked Jill.

"All the biggest and best in England," replied Mrs. Payne promptly. "By the way," she went on, "he's no beginner's pony; he's keen, you know, and needs some holding."

"That's all right; I'll be able to manage him, and I would much rather have something a bit on the hot side than behind the bit," said Jill.

"Anyway," said Aunt Margaret, "Jill's an accomplished young horsewoman, and if he pulls she will be able to re-school him."

By this time we had reached the stable, and Mrs. Payne opened the top door. We all looked in and saw a heavily built, dappled grey with a roman nose and hogged mane.

"Come on, Topper, old man, stand properly," said Mrs. Payne, making him stand with equal weight on all four feet.

Jill ran a critical eye over him. "He looks rather common after Sunshine," she said.

"It's not always the breedy ones that make the jumpers," said Mrs. Payne.

36

He shot forward.

"I know that, but he doesn't look as though he has much scope," said Jill.

"Could you put a saddle on, so that we can see him jump?" said Aunt Margaret.

"Certainly, but unfortunately my son is still recovering from appendicitis so he can't show him off, but perhaps your daughter would like to jump him herself," said Mrs. Payne. Then she fetched the tack and put it on.

The bridle had a drop noseband and the bit was an ordinary, jointed snaffle, but she put on a tight, running martingale as well, and so made it quite severe. This done she led Topper out, and into a paddock behind the stable.

She held him while Jill mounted and adjusted her

stirrups. Then, saying cheerfully, "Off you go," she took her hand from the rein. Topper leapt forward; Jill pulled him up and tried to make him walk, but he danced about, giving little snorts, and after a few moments Mrs. Payne suggested that Jill should jump him over a very solid-looking gate of about four feet high, with enormous wings. Jill said, in disapproving tones, that she had hardly loosened his muscles, but that she supposed she might as well. Then, with an angry frown, she turned him towards it; he shot forward and before Jill had collected her wits together, he had galloped past.

"Well, I never," said Mrs. Payne. "He has never done that with John."

"Are you insinuating that it was my daughter's fault he refused?" asked Aunt Margaret, with a little toss of her head.

"No, not at all; she's all right—she only needs to get used to him and they will be taking all the prizes," said Mrs. Payne in calm, slow accents.

"Try again," shouted Stephen.

Jill turned Topper at the jump again, but to my surprise exactly the same thing happened.

"I'll lean it and make it lower. Really I don't know why he's running out like this, he's never done it before," said Mrs. Payne.

"He needs re-schooling," said Jill.

Then she rode him at the gate, but the same thing happened once again, only this time she was leaning too far forward when she pulled him up, and he chucked his head up and hit her on the nose. It began to bleed and Jill gave a wail. Aunt Margaret said, "My poor pet," and ran to her. "Are you all right, dear?" she asked.

"It's bleeding," said Jill, and she burst into tears.

"Hullo," said Mrs. Payne in jolly tones, arriving on the spot. "Had a knock? That happened to me once out hunting just after I had jumped some stiff timber on an ex-steeplechaser. He was the dickens of a puller, but one of the boldest horses I've ever met—would jump anything, you know, didn't matter what the take-off was, mud or stones he would go over just the same."

"Feeling better now, dear?" asked Aunt Margaret.

"I'm feeling sick and the beastly thing won't stand still," said Jill, trying to blow her nose while Topper danced about, and sidled, and snorted.

"Hold on to him, Stephen, while Jill gets off," said Aunt Margaret. "He's not at all what we wanted. We were looking for a really super jumper," she said to Mrs. Payne.

Mrs. Payne said, "He is that all right, and I'm sorry that your daughter can't manage him, but I *did* tell you he wasn't suitable for a beginner."

"I'm not a beginner. Lord Langley says I am quite exceptional. It's your pony that's wrong, he's the worst-mannered thing I've ever ridden," said Jill furiously.

"So there!" added Stephen, in what I call his prep-school voice.

"Do you realise that we have come thirty miles for nothing?" asked Aunt Margaret.

"You advertised for a pony for a super rider and if your daughter is not so super as you thought, it's your look-out, I'm afraid," said Mrs. Payne, taking Topper from Stephen.

"I don't know how you dare to say such a thing when everybody knows that Jill is one of the best riders in the country—Lord Stanwell said so himself and he ought to know," said Aunt Margaret.

"A fat lot he knows," said Mrs. Payne.

"Come on, children, we will go home now," said Aunt Margaret, doing her best to sound dignified.

We walked back through the garden to the car in a dreary silence, only broken now and then by an indignant sniff from Jill.

The journey home was long and very dismal. Except for Stephen saying that trying the pony was a swizz and Aunt Margaret occasionally saying, "Better now, dear?" to Jill, no one spoke.

We arrived back in time for a late tea of stale scones and raspberry jam. I had a fit of clumsiness, which was very tactless considering that every one was in a bad temper. First I upset my tea and burned Jill's hand, then I dropped the jam spoon on the white tablecloth, making a dirty, jammy mark. Aunt Margaret seized the opportunity to give vent to her temper and lectured me on my carelessness, bad manners and general uncouthness for a long time. Did I behave like that when I was out to tea? she asked. I only said that I was sorry, because it is no use annoying grown-ups especially when they are in bad tempers; but I felt angry and disagreeable, and I had an awful, babyish longing to run out of the room and slam the door.

When tea was over I wrote to Mummy and told her all about the fire and going to Steadley Green, which took three pages; and it was dinner-time when I had finished. At dinner I tried to be particularly well mannered, but Aunt Margaret was in far too bad a temper to notice, and sent us all to bed directly afterwards.

Next morning after breakfast something exciting happened. I was walking through the hall on my way out to see the ponies, when I heard a knock at the front door and, knowing by the time that it was the

40

postman—probably with a parcel—and thinking that I might save some one some trouble, I opened it. I was right. The postman was there, but instead of handing me a parcel he gave me a registered letter addressed to myself, and a slip to sign to show that I had got it. When he had gone, I put the other letters, which were all for my aunt, on the hall chest and opened mine. Inside I found fifteen pound notes. I expect you can guess my surprise. For a moment I thought that I must have made a mistake and that it wasn't for me, but I looked again and there was Miss Augusta Thorndyke written clearly enough for any one. Then I turned the envelope inside out and a letter fell out; it said:

Dear Augusta,—I shall be very grateful if you will accept this small present in return for so gallantly saving my farm from being destroyed by fire. I hope you will find something nice to spend it on. Please do not bother to thank me for this which is very little in comparison with what you have done for me. Your ever grateful servant, James Houseman.

I read the letter twice and then, stuffing it and the money into my pocket, I ran upstairs to the nursery to tell my cousins. They were all leaning over the wireless, which had something wrong with it as usual.

"Look what I've been sent," I said, plunging my hands into my pocket. No one took any notice.

"Look, isn't it lovely. I know what I shall spend it on," I said.

"Sssh," said Barbara.

"I shall keep it and spend it on my pony," I said obstinately.

"Shut up," said Jill, giving the wireless a tap.

"You are beastly, you *might* look," I said.

"For goodness' sake shut-up," said Stephen. "Can't you see that we are trying to mend the wireless. *We* want to hear *Strange Passage* to-night even if you don't."

"Sssh, it hummed," said Barbara.

"All right, you shan't see and serves you right too," I said, walking out of the room and slamming the door.

I went into my bedroom and put the money and letter into my handkerchief case; then I sat on my bed and lost myself in thought. . . . Of course, I knew what I would spend the money on; the trouble was that nice ponies cost more than fifteen pounds—Jill had told me that anything costing less than sixty was sure to be pretty awful—and I had no hope of getting more money. Anyway, I didn't want to wait. On second thoughts, though, I decided that I would rather have a "pretty awful pony" than no pony. After all, he would *be* a pony, and I would be able to ride, and Jill had called Dominoe awful, but I had enjoyed riding him. I might be able to school and improve my pony, too. Teach him to jump, perhaps. One of my cousins' books said that *all* ponies are natural jumpers, I remembered. Gradually I became more hopeful until I was finally imagining myself winning the children's jumping at Olympia. I even heard Aunt Margaret's surprised, "Well done, Augusta, what a superb round." And Stephen's, "My, can't he jump?"

Perhaps it was a good thing that my fantastic dreams were at last interrupted by Aunt Margaret calling my name.

"Coming," I shouted, and I jumped up off my bed and ran downstairs. She was in the morning-room reading the paper. "What is it?" I asked.

"Nothing, only I wondered whether anything was the matter. It seems rather queer to sit alone in a bedroom in the middle of the morning," she said.

"Yes, it is," I said. I am sure that I irritated Aunt Margaret, but I had suddenly realised that she might not let me keep a pony, and the thought was at once horrible and disappointing. For a moment, I think, my mind was a blank; vaguely I heard my aunt say something about some one being ill, but I didn't listen. I made up my mind to tell her everything, then and there.

"I say," I said.

"Augusta! It is very rude not to answer when people speak to you, and you are quite old enough to know that," said Aunt Margaret.

"I'm sorry! I didn't hear you. What *did* you say?" I asked.

"Really, Augusta, how can you tell such lies? You *must* have heard—I asked you whether you were ill."

"Gosh! No. Why should I be?" I said, wondering if I had better show her the money and letter before telling how I had got them.

"You seem to behave so queerly," she said.

I was wondering whether the moment was suitable for telling all, and I glanced at my aunt without answering; she looked formidable and angry, and I funked and decided to leave it to lunch-time. Then I realised that she expected me to say something.

"Oh, dear, I'm sorry," I said.

"I can see you are," she said sarcastically.

"Where are the others?" I asked.

"They went out for a ride some time ago. I don't know why you don't sometimes go with them on one of the cycles, instead of always moping about with a book," she said.

"Yes, I might," I said, walking out of the room.

"What are you going to do now?" asked Aunt Margaret.

"Read," I said; then realising that I had been tactless, I added, "out of doors, in the sunshine, in the fresh air."

"I see," she said, starting to read the paper.

I went up to the nursery and borrowed one of my cousins' instructive, horsey books, which has a chapter on buying horses at a low price. I went out into the garden and sat down on the lawn, and started to read. A few minutes later I heard a tap at the morning-room window, and Aunt Margaret shouted that I wasn't to sit on the damp grass. I moved on to the garden seat and went on with my reading. I found the book rather disheartening, because the author considered fifty pounds a low price and suggested that, if the prospective buyer could only afford such a sum, he should buy a horse either with only one eye or "deficient eyesight." He added that the horse which was second in the Grand National in 1927 was completely blind in one eye, so that one could easily afford to take the risks of a little lack of vision in a hunter.

As I expect you can imagine, I did not like this suggestion, and the worst of it was that I had only fifteen pounds and so obviously I couldn't ignore it. The very thought of this spoiled all my plans. For already I had decided what my pony would be like—a dark brown, bay or grey if possible. He would have plenty of splints and spavins in suitable places for them to make no difference to his soundness, and he might have a capped hock if necessary, or be nervous in traffic or slow; but always I had seen him with a small intelligent head and large kind eyes, and the very

44

thought that I might have to come down to buying a pony with only one eye sank me in gloom.

I stopped reading the book, but when lunch time came I was still feeling pessimistic. This I suppose was what suddenly made me feel certain that Aunt Margaret wouldn't let me keep a pony, even if I was terribly tactful and polite. It was with a funny feeling at the pit of my stomach, that I walked into the dining-room for lunch and sat down.

When every one had started eating Aunt Margaret asked my cousins whether they had had a nice ride, and they replied, "Yes, very, thank you." Then silence fell and I told myself that now was my chance, but somehow I couldn't make myself start, and although I had thought frantically, I had said nothing when Aunt Margaret broke the silence by asking my cousins what they proposed to do during the afternoon.

"I dunno," said Stephen.

"Well," said Aunt Margaret brightly, "I'm going into Dilford, and one of you might bring your wireless, then we can have it mended, and Augusta, you had better come too, so that I can buy you a decent hat; I can't have you going to church like that again."

"O.K. Thank you very much," I said.

"Fains go with the wireless," said Jill.

"Fains," said Barbara quickly.

"You'll have to go, Stephen," said Jill.

"Pig," said Stephen.

Again there was silence. I took the plunge. "Do you know——?" I said.

"I have been telling Augusta that she ought to go out with you on your rides on one of the bikes," said Aunt Margaret. "It would be much nicer than moping at home."

"I don't think it would," said Barbara. "After all,

45

it's not much fun riding a bicycle down lanes and across fields, especially if its owner doesn't want it punctured. What she needs is a dog-quiet pony to potter about on."

Ignoring Barbara's last contemptuous sentence, I quickly said to my aunt, "If I was given or got a pony would you let me keep it here if I bought the oats and hay?"

"Yes, you certainly can and naturally I would pay for the food," said Aunt Margaret, in one of her rare good tempers.

"Ponies don't only need hay and oats, you know, Augusta; they need bran and chaff, and grass and shoes, as well," said Jill.

"Thank you very much," I said to Aunt Margaret. "What for," she asked.

"Saying that if I get a pony you will pay for his food," I said.

"Well, I don't for a moment think that you *will* be given a pony, so I shouldn't be too hopeful," she said.

"Decent ponies are never given away—they are worth too much. That is why there is the old saying, 'Never look a gift horse in the mouth,' " said Jill.

"Quite right, Jill," said Aunt Margaret.

By then we had finished lunch and Stephen asked whether we could leave the table. My aunt said that we could, and I found *Horse and Hound,* and looked at the advertisements of ponies for sale. They all sounded lovely, but the cheapest was twenty-five pounds, and I began to feel gloomy again.

Later in the afternoon I went into Dilford with Aunt Margaret and Stephen. Aunt Margaret bought me a very smug-looking, crushed strawberry hat, and told me that I was to wear it when I next went to church or went out.

46

On the way home we stopped at a garage to get some petrol, and I noticed that there were a great many pens behind the inn, opposite. I asked Stephen what they were for, and he said that cattle and pigs were sold there every Saturday, and, occasionally, one or two old, thin or vicious horses and ponies. This, of course, interested me and I asked him whether he knew of anybody ever buying a good pony there. He said that he certainly didn't as only half-witted people bought ponies from markets like that. I said were they all useless or were there sometimes horses merely suffering from worms, which could be cured? And he said that he didn't know and why did I want to know, anyway? I said, "I just wondered."

Then Aunt Margaret paid for the petrol and we drove home.

We found Jill in great excitement, because a reply to her advertisement in *Horse and Hound* had come by the afternoon post. Apparently, a man named Tom Smithers had a trained jumper called High Jinks for sale, which had already won three cups and ten pounds in prize money in children's jumping classes during April.

"That sounds more like the type of thing we want," said Aunt Margaret. "How much is he asking?"

"A hundred and thirty," Jill replied.

All that evening there was the same sort of talk as there had been about the grey—what Susan Phillips and John Dunlop would say when Jill beat them, what tests she would give High Jinks to see whether he was broken-winded or a whistler or roarer; and so on. I felt less and less like telling them about my fifteen pounds. I knew they would laugh to scorn my ridiculous idea of buying a pony for so small a sum, even if I did tell them that I was willing to put up with one with a missing eye.

After dinner Aunt Margaret rang up Tom Smithers and arranged to see High Jinks on the following Saturday. It meant a long journey by car and she planned to start early. Stephen would be back at school, but Barbara and Jill were not going back to the Monday, and as I was going to their school, I wasn't either; so Aunt Margaret included me in the party.

While I lay in bed that night I realised that I did not want to go and see High Jinks—it would probably end with disagreeable words again, anyway, I thought. I wanted much more to go to Dilford Market and buy a pony for fifteen pounds—never mind if he was thin or vicious, I should have to put up with that.

Late into the night I tried to think of excuses, which Aunt Margaret would be likely to accept, for me not going to see High Jinks; but all in vain, and by next morning I was sunk in dark despair. Then, just before breakfast I decided that I would pretend to feel sick as we were about to leave. I hoped that Aunt Margaret would tell me to rest on my bed, and then go without me. I wouldn't really be telling a lie, I decided, because most likely I would be feeling vaguely sick with excitement. Anyway, I could eat very little for dinner the night before, and if I ate very little for breakfast on the morning, too, I would feel sick with hunger. Then directly they had left I would catch the Dilford bus—I had often seen it stop a little way up the road—and go to the market.

This decided, I waited with great impatience for Saturday. Time seemed to pass incredibly slowly, but at last the great day came and, as we were having breakfast at half-past seven, I jumped out of bed

48

I waited in agonies of apprehension.

directly I was called. I quickly washed and dressed, putting on my best shirt, sleeveless pullover and tie, and also my only pair of jodphurs, which were sadly the worse for wear, being patched and dirty. Then whistling gaily, I ran down stairs to the dining-room. Aunt Margaret was already there, and she was giving the cook some orders; she stopped when she saw me and after giving my clothes one disgusted glance, told me that I was to go straight upstairs, take off those shabby jodhs, put on my least untidy skirt and tweed coat, brush my hair, and put on my new hat after breakfast.

"O.K.," I said, and I ran upstairs and did as she asked, feeling quite cheerful because I knew that I could change back before leaving for Dilford Market.

I ate very little breakfast, because of seeming and feeling sick, but no one noticed. Then at half-past eight, when we were about to start, I said that I was feeling sick—it was true, too; my efforts had not been in vain. Aunt Margaret said that she had better take my temperature, and I hastily said that I didn't think I had one. She felt my forehead and said that it didn't seem very hot, but that it was best to be on the safe side. She fetched the thermometer and of course my temperature was normal. Jill said that I was a fusspot and Aunt Margaret said that I had better lie on my bed, and that they would have to go without me.

"Bad luck, Augusta," said Barbara.

I tried to look disappointed and, feeling an awful hypocrite, walked slowly up to my bedroom.

After that everything was easy. I caught the bus, when I had waited at the stop for about twenty minutes, without mishap, and paid my fare of five-pence with some pocket money which I had saved.

When I reached the market, I found only one or two cows in a few pens and I felt sure that, somehow, Stephen or I must have made a mistake. I am sorry to say that I began to wish that I had gone to see High Jinks after all. I waited in agonies of apprehension for what seemed like an age and then, to my relief, I heard moo-ing and shouting. Soon a herd of

50

bullocks arrived and ten pens were filled up by them. I asked one of the men, who had been driving them, when the sale began. He laughed, and said had I come to buy bullocks? Then, not waiting for an answer, he said that it began at twelve o'clock and that the time was half-past nine. I thanked him and talked to the bullocks. Some were red and others black; they all had white heads and short, blunt horns. It was horrible to think that soon they would all be slaughtered for the sake of human stomachs—to satisfy human greed. I looked at the bullocks for some time, and then I decided to see whether I could teach one of them to shake hands like Dominoe. I had no food to use as rewards, so I went out into the street and found a baker's shop. I bought three bread rolls, and paid for them with the rest of my saved pocket money. Then I chose the tamest bullock—he was a black one—and after naming him Warrior, started his education. I did not find him such an intelligent pupil as Dominoe, but I think he was beginning to decide that he was supposed to pick up his foot when I tapped his leg, when I noticed that some ponies had been tied up in a pen over the other side of the market. I hastily gave Warrior the rest of the bread rolls and ran across, and looked at the ponies; there were three of them, a fat, iron-grey and two thin bays. The bays were nondescript—the sort of ponies you wouldn't easily recognise if you met them pulling a cart—and they were rather alike. Both had black points and coarse heads; both were heavily built; neither had any white, but one was a gelding and a little taller, and straighter in the shoulder than the other, which was a mare.

The grey was different. He was fat and shiny, young and lively, and his back looked short and strong in contrast with the hollow one of his tired comrades.

his head was dark grey with a white star and below the star was a broad white race, which gave him a dashing appearance; in a way, it resembled Sunshine's head, with the same broad forehead and cheek, and fine tapering nose. But what struck me most about him were his eyes; large, liquid, brown, they looked as soft as velvet and yet their brightness reminded me of friendly stars breaking through a dark sky at night. I tried not to look at him because I knew that he would fetch more than fifteen pounds, and I talked to the other ponies. They were not very pleased—I expect they hated humans of all kinds and I don't blame them.

Gradually the empty pens were filled by pigs and cattle, and soon there was quite a crowd of people. A broken-down carthorse was tied near the ponies. He looked old and tired, and I wished that I had not given all my bread to Warrior.

I heard some distant clock strike eleven and I decided to see if I could tell the ponies' ages. The bay gelding had a disappearing Galvayne's groove and I supposed that he must be over twenty. The mare's teeth were quite different; the centrals were worn down, nearly to the gum and I could not think why. Only later did I find out that she must have been a crib-biter. The carthorse seemed the oldest; his teeth were very long and he had no sign of the Galvayne's groove, but the grey had the nicest of them all; his were clean and short, and I knew that he was still in the prime of life.

After looking at their ages I felt their legs and nearly was kicked by the mare, which had heat in her near hind. All except the grey had very filled legs, and the bay gelding had two splints, and the carthorse seemed to be starting ringbone. While I was feeling

the grey's legs he gently took the smug hat—in my
haste to leave the house and catch the bus, I had forgotten to change after all—from my head and started
to chew it. Only after the greatest difficulty did I per-
suade him to leave go and by then the wretched thing
was covered in slobber. I can't think what Aunt Margaret would have said if she had seen it, but, as you
will find out if you read on, she was fated never to
look on it again.

Soon I heard the distant clock strike twelve and
every one, but me, seemed to hurry over to the other
end of the market. I stayed where I was, because I
knew nothing of sales and was frightened that if I
moved from the ponies I might miss seeing them sold.
Two men, hurrying with the rest, stopped as they were
about to pass me. One of them pointed a finger at the
grey and, winking, asked the other how much he was
going to bid for Jackson's pony.

"The same as old Charlie paid for 'is boots," replied
the other; then they both laughed and hurried on.

CHAPTER FOUR

A NICE-LOOKING six-year-old, broken to riding, but
with no warranty, was how the auctioneer described
the grey pony when at long last he was brought up for
sale. Led by a boy, he was trotted up the passage between two rows of pens. To me, he looked lovely,
ideal, perfect, the very image of what I had always
wanted. I wished that I had a hundred and thirty
pounds to spend; I knew that I would not hesitate to
53

buy him then, unless he cost more—of course, that was possible.

The first bid came from a fat man in a dust coat. "I'll bid five," he said.

"Five I'm bid," said the auctioneer.

"Six," said some one.

"Seven," said some one else.

The fat man in the dust coat nodded to the auctioneer who promptly said, "Eight."

The the bidding stopped and the auctioneer said wasn't anybody going to give more for this fine, up-standing pony?

"Nine," I said, loudly and clearly. Every one seemed to turn and look at me.

"Ten," said the man in the dust coat.

"Eleven," I said.

Some one prodded me. "I shouldn't buy that grey, miss, he's——"

"Twelve I'm bid."

And I hastily said, "Thirteen."

Again there was silence; my heart leapt. Surely I was not going to get him.

"Thirteen, I'm bid. Come on now, gentlemen; don't let him sell at an unlucky price," said the auctioneer.

The man in the dust coat looked at the grey's teeth and ran a hand down his legs. "Fourteen," he said.

"Fifteen," I said, my voice sounding higher than usual.

I waited; I knew that in a moment a voice would say sixteen. Then all would be over for me; I would not have the grey. Some one else would have him.

The silence was broken, but by the auctioneer; he asked incredulously whether there were no more bids and then, after waiting a few minutes, he banged down the hammer, and said, "Name, please?"

I could not answer him; amazing though it may seem, I had forgotten my name. For a moment I thought that I had gone mad, then I remembered. "Augusta Thorndyke," I said.

"Thank you," he said.

The grey was led back into his pen, and I asked a good-natured looking man where I paid. He explained the way to the office and as I wended my way through the crowd in that direction, I counted my money. I had not lost any; there was still fifteen pounds. The office was full of people and I had to wait. I thought how awful it would be if, by some ghastly mistake, I had bid fifty pounds. What would I do? I wondered. My suspense was ended by the man behind the counter saying: "Yes, miss?"

I said, "Oh, look, here's the money for the grey."

"What is the lot number?" he asked.

"A hundred and two," I told him, pushing the money across the counter.

He looked through his papers and counted the notes. Then to my absolute horror, he said, "fifteen shillings short, I'm afraid."

"But," I said, "I have given you fifteen pounds."

"Yes," he said; "but the pony was sold for guineas, *not* pounds." I remember those words made me feel strangely sick. They seemed to put an end to everything. For a moment I thought I was going to cry, but I forced back the tears, and saying, "All right, I'll go and get some more money," in what I hoped were convincing tones, I dashed out of the office. I ran right out into the street and then I pulled up, and leaned against a lamp-post. My legs felt suddenly weak, and I still had that strange sick feeling.

I am afraid that I am not one of those gifted people who staunchly say, "Never say die," in the darkest moments; instead I always think the worst and become plunged in gloom. While I leaned against the lamp-post, I certainly saw the worst. . . . Horrible men leading my pony away to be destroyed, policemen coming to arrest me for pretending to have money that I did not possess, Aunt Margaret banishing me from Tree Tops for ever; all these scenes I saw clearly in my imagination, and they added to my gloom. I am sorry to say that in a very few minutes I was crying steadily. Then, to make matters worse, it began to rain, not slightly, but in big, ugly drops—the kind which will soak through a coat in no time. Soon my hair was wet and I remembered that I had the smug hat in my pocket. With a wave of bitterness, I realised that it had cost fifteen shillings; then I had an idea. It was that I should sell the hat to a second-hand clothes' shop. I knew that I wouldn't get as much as I wanted for it, but I told myself that every little bit would help. With a lighter heart, I scanned the smoke-grimed street and, although I saw no second-hand clothes' shops, I noticed a man turning the corner at the end and pushing a builder's hand-cart. I tore after him and, catching up, said, "Please, is there a second-hand clothes' dealer anywhere near here?"

He looked at me in amazement for a moment, and then said, "Keep straight on and take the second turning to the left, and you'll find one at the end of the street—you can't miss it."

"Thanks awfully," I said, and ran on.

I found the shop quite easily; it had J. E. SMITH in large letters above the window, which was littered with old shoes, tobacco pouches, watches, dingy coats and such like. I gazed at them for a few moments, and then, filled with trepidation, I opened the door and walked in. I was greeted by the mingled smell of boiled cabbage, linoleum and old clothes. I waited; all seemed silent; in a wave of impatience, I hit the counter with my fist. Somewhere in a room behind a baby cried; then all was silent again. I scraped the floor with my feet and opened the bell-less door and slammed it shut. I was wasting time, it seemed. Won't anybody come, I wondered. Then, to my joy, I heard footsteps and a woman in an overall came through the door behind the counter.

"Can I help you, miss?" she said.

I remember that I was terribly relieved; I had been expecting to have to deal with a dark man with ear-rings and a whining, gipsy voice. The woman I saw was quite ordinary—perhaps she was a little dirtier than the average shopkeeper's wife, but that was all.

Feeling much more hopeful, I asked her whether she would like to bury a practically new hat. I produced mine, which looked incredibly dirty, considering that it had only been worn once. She did not look at it; instead she stared at me. Then she said, "What have you been up to, young lady; got into trouble with mother?"

"No. I don't like this hat, and I want to get rid of it and I want to sell it, because I want some money," I said.

"I'll give you half a crown," she said.

"That's no good. It's worth much more," I said.

"Let me see it," she said, and took the smug hat out of my hands. "It's crumpled and dirty and doesn't look new, but if I cleaned it up I suppose some one might take a fancy to it for their kiddie. I'll give you three and sixpence," she said.

"O.K.," I said; "but I want to sell these too." I took off my tie and pullover, and handed them across the counter.

"I want to sell these too."

"What have you been up to, my dear?" she said. "Not in debt at your age, I hope."

"How much will you give me for them?" I said, wondering what else I could sell to get fifteen shillings. "The tie's cashmere," I added, just in case it made any difference.

"Well, it's dingy, too, and this woolly is darned and faded, but I could let you have two and a tanner for the two," she said, looking me straight in the face.

That only made six shillings—less than half the amount I needed—and I desperately tried to think what else I could sell. Then suddenly I knew—the silver buttons on my coat. It seemed a pity to have to part with them, because Mummy had given them to me when I was six. They had been on several different coats of mine since then, and I had grown fond of them, as one can of many things that one has had a long time; but I ruthlessly told myself that people who bought ponies in secret must expect to have to make sacrifices, and asked the woman for a knife. She looked rather taken aback—I believe that she thought I was going to try and commit suicide, for a moment; then she shrugged her shoulders and fetched a kitchen knife from the room behind the shop. She gave it to me, and I swiftly cut two silver buttons off my coat. Then I put them on the counter and told her that she could have them, the hat, the pullover and the tie for fifteen shillings, but she laughed, and pointed out that the buttons were bent and battered.

"Well, how much *will* you pay me?" I asked desperately.

"Twelve and six," she said.

"Gosh, you are mean. You know perfectly well that you can sell the hat alone for that," I said angrily, for I felt bitterly disappointed.

She looked at me hard in the face again; then she smiled, and said, "All right, dear. I can see you are a plucky kid. I'll give you your fifteen shillings for the lot."

"Oh, thank you; thanks awfully," I said. For,
59

although I knew that they must be worth much more, I felt frightfully pleased because nothing seemed to matter, except that I could have my pony, my own grey pony.

The woman opened an old tobacco tin full of money, and counted fifteen shillings in silver. She handed it to me and I thanked her and dashed out of her shop. In the street the air seemed fresh and sweet, after the stuffy smell of old clothes, and I whistled as I ran back to the market.

The same man was in the office and he looked surprised to see me—I expect that he noticed my pullover and tie and buttons were missing. I gave him the money and he counted it before giving me a receipt and a slip of paper, which he said I was to hand to the man at the entrance when I went out with my purchase. I thanked him and left the office.

My pony was still in the same pen, but his comrades had gone. He whinnied when he saw me and I patted his sleek, grey neck and told him that he was mine for ever and ever. Then I untied him and led him out of the market, giving the man at the entrance the pass on my way.

Once out on the road, I was glad to find that my pony was quiet in traffic—two huge lorries passed us and he didn't turn a hair. I kept on patting his neck, because he looked so beautiful, and I felt very proud of him. While I walked along I thought of how surprised my cousins would be when I arrived home with such a good-looking grey pony. I felt sure that they would not believe that he came from Dilford Market and, of course, they would want to know where I had scraped up the money. It would be fun telling them about the fire; most likely they would be a little sceptical at first, but I would show them Captain House-

He looked like a dream.

man's letter and that would settle their doubts. They
would think that I was queer not telling them before,
but Aunt Margaret would be pleased because she

would know that I wouldn't mope about with a book if I had a pony—or would she? Would she be pleased? . . . Suddenly I realised that they might have arrived back at Tree Tops some time ago, that they might be wondering where I was—searching for me. It was as though a dark cloud had blotted out the sun that had shone so brightly only a moment before; for now my mind was filled with dread and I had awful visions of Aunt Margaret ringing up the Police Station and telling whoever answered to scour the countryside for a little girl (she always speaks of me as a *little girl* although, actually, I am not small for my age) with dark hair and a crushed strawberry-coloured hat. Every moment I expected a police car to draw up beside me or Aunt Margaret to appear round the next corner. But time passed and I saw neither, and soon I began to look at my pony again and he looked like a dream, as he strode along with ears pricked and head high, and I knew that to have him was worth risking all Aunt Margaret's anger.

I started to whistle again because the sight of him made me feel happy and then, when I was right out of the suburbs of Dilford, I scrambled from off a bank on to his back and rode along. He felt heavenly, not as broad as Dominoe, but very tall and strong, and his stride seemed longer and his carriage gayer than any pony that I had ridden before. I told him that he was wonderful, and the apple of my eye, and then I tried to invent poetry about him.

This is as far as I got:

> My pony, which I bought to-day,
> Has a shiny coat of smoky grey,
> And his star that is so pearly white
> Will help me see him in the night.

My pony, which I bought in town,
Has large, brown eyes of darkish brown
Which shine with joy and sheer delight
And never roll in angry spite.

My pony, which I bought alone,
Has lovely hocks and good, thick bone,
A head both small and finely cut . . .

I couldn't think of a suitable rhyme for cut, so I gave up my poem which, perhaps, was a good thing, because, as you see, it didn't scan and I don't think it was worthy of my pony. Instead I started whistling and then I turned off on to the Fledgewood road, which has a grass verge, and told my pony to trot. Although I was riding bareback, his trot seemed smooth and, as I did not feel at all like falling off, I cantered him as well and that was lovely, too.

A few minutes later, I rode up the back drive of Tree Tops. Nobody was about, but I was glad to see that the car was in the garage—obviously Aunt Margaret was not anxiously searching for me. I turned my pony out into the field and the others, in the stable, called to him. He answered, and his neigh was loud and shrill. I watched him as he walked across to speak to them; in the greyness of the twilight, he looked more phantom than real. It was with reluctance that I turned at last and went slowly up the path to the house.

I opened the garden door and walked into the dining-room; here all was still and the very quietness made my mind fill with dread. . . . She will be furious, I thought; and my heart failed me and I sat down on one of the heavy Jacobean chairs, which look so out of place in Aunt Margaret's middling house, and became wrapt in gloom.

I don't know how long I sat there—it may have been only a few minutes or perhaps nearly an hour—but I remember that I wished that I was back at Blenheim Cottage, and that I couldn't take my eyes off the long row of silver cups on the mantelpiece. Every one had been won by Jill, who in a few minutes was to know about the beautiful grey pony which was mine. . . . What will she think of him? Supposing she finds that he has a broken wind or navicular. What shall I say then? I wondered.

Suddenly the stillness was broken by the sound of footsteps—some one was coming downstairs. Then a voice rang out; it was Jill's.

"Mummy, she's not here," she shouted.

Aunt Margaret answered from the drawing-room. "All right, come back and finish your tea. I dare say she's gone out for a walk on her own; probably she will innocently turn up at dinner time. I wouldn't put it past her—and there's no point in worrying unduly till then."

"Well, Mrs. Smith and Betty say that they haven't seen her all day," said Jill.

Then I heard the drawing-room door shut and, after that, only the muffled sound of voices and the clink of cups and saucers. Obviously they had arrived home a few minutes before me and were now having a late tea. Aunt Margaret seemed in a good temper, judging by the tone of her voice, and I told myself that now was the time to take the plunge and tell her all. I stood up; I heard Mrs. Smith in the kitchen, preparing the dinner. In a moment Susan, the parlour-maid, would come in and lay the table; she would be surprised to find me standing alone in the growing darkness; she would think that I was "queer."

"Come on," I said to myself. "Now or never."

I walked through the hall and opened the drawing-room door and went in. They were all there—Aunt Margaret, Barbara and Jill, and when they saw me they stopped talking. Suddenly I felt rather sick and very hungry and completely tongue-tied; surely some one will speak, I thought.

"Well?" said Aunt Margaret at last.

"Sorry I'm late," I said.

"What on earth have you been doing with yourself? Mrs. Smith says you were so quiet she forgot you were here, and didn't give you any lunch or tea. Why didn't you go and *ask* her for something to eat? Really, you are a queer child," said Aunt Margaret.

"I didn't want anything," I replied, quite truthfully.

"We were getting quite worried about you," Aunt Margaret went on. "You know, it's very naughty of you to wander around at this time of night, especially when you know we are out."

"We've bought him," said Jill.

"Who?" I asked, absent-mindedly.

"High Jinks—he's marvellous and can clear six foot. I rode him, and he gave me a much better feel than that other straight-shouldered animal. I should think I can hardly *not* be in the money on a pony like him," said Jill.

"Yes, I shouldn't wonder if you get to Olympia," said Aunt Margaret. "*And* take first in the jumping, during next season."

"What *will* John Dunlop say?" said Jill.

"I've bought a pony, too," I said. "He's awfully nice and a grey."

They all stared at me in amazement; then Aunt

65

Margaret said, "What on earth are you talking about?"

For a moment I felt like giggling, but I reminded myself that this was a matter of life or death. "It is true, I bought him from Dilford Market for fifteen guineas," I said, and I tried to make my tone convincing.

"May I ask, who gave you permission to go out for the day?" said Aunt Margaret.

"Where is the pony?" said Barbara.

"When's the Dublin Show, Mummy?" interrupted Jill.

"Be quiet. I want to get this straight," said Aunt Margaret. "What is all this nonsense about buying a pony, Augusta?"

"I bought one to-day; he's in your field now—that's all right, isn't it?" I said.

"From Dilford Market?" queried Jill.

"And from where, may I ask, did the money come?" said Aunt Margaret.

"Captain Houseman," I replied.

"Captain Houseman," echoed Jill.

"Honestly, you are queer. What will you be saying next?" said Barbara.

"Now look here, Augusta, either you stop talking nonsense and tell the truth or you go straight to bed," threatened Aunt Margaret. I began to giggle and I believe that, then, they really thought that I had gone mad, for they looked at me curiously and Aunt Margaret's tone changed. "Calm yourself and try to speak the truth," she said.

"I'm quite calm, thank you, and I am not lying. Captain Houseman gave me fifteen pounds, because I saved one of his farms from being burnt to the ground," I said.

66

"Impossible! He is the most disagreeable man in the district and would certainly never think of giving a little girl like you fifteen pounds," said Aunt Margaret.

"I don't believe you," said Jill.

"O.K. Wait a minute," I shouted. I ran out of the room and upstairs to my bedroom. I seized Captain Houseman's letter from out of my handkerchief-case and ran back. I handed it to Aunt Margaret. She read in silence and the others watched her as though entranced. Then she finished and looked up.

"And you accepted it?" she said.

"Yes, and spent the money on a pony," I replied.

"Let me see," said Jill, snatching the letter.

"In fact, you have been deliberately deceitful," said Aunt Margaret, and I could tell by her tone that she was angry.

"No, I wanted to tell you," I said, "but you were always talking about Jill's pony, and I could never get a word in and—well, I wanted to choose mine by myself," I finished up untruthfully, for as you know, that wasn't the reason, but somehow I couldn't explain how difficult telling them had seemed. I knew that they wouldn't understand or believe me.

"Oh, did you?" said Aunt Margaret. "Now I know why you thanked me so profusely when I said that you could keep a pony here. I suppose you were planning then. Really, Augusta, of all the deceitful——"

"Let's go and see the pony," interrupted Barbara.

"Yes, he must be pretty awful if he cost fifteen guineas," said Jill.

"We will do not such thing. Augusta, you have been a very naughty little girl, and you are to go to bed immediately without any supper," said Aunt Margaret; "and I shall write to your mother to-night," she added.

"I have told her about the fire," I said.

Then I slowly walked out of the room and upstairs to bed.

I did not sleep well that night. I was hungry (although Aunt Margaret broke her word and sent Betty, one of the maids, up with a glass of milk and four sweet biscuits), and I knew that next day was Sunday; and because I had no hat, that was not a nice thing to know.

CHAPTER FIVE

WHEN I wakened in the morning, I heard the birds singing and, on looking out of my bedroom window, I found that day was breaking. I jumped out of bed, and dressed quickly, and, carrying my shoes, I crept downstairs, and let myself out into the garden. Then I ran down the path to the field—and there was my pony. I could only see him dimly, because it was not yet light, but even in the mistiness of the early morning he looked marvellous. He was cropping the short spring grass, by the stable. I called to him and he lifted his head and gazed at me, but he did not move in my direction, and soon started to graze again. I climbed on to the gate of the field and sat and watched him, and thought about the none-too-rosy future. This did me little good, except that I decided one important thing—my pony's name. I chose to call him Daybreak, partly because he was the right colour, and partly because the daybreak of that morning was

I chose to call him Daybreak.

particularly beautiful, but mostly because I liked the sound of it and that, after all, is what matters in a name.

I walked across the field and told my pony that he was now called Daybreak, but I think he was really more interested in the grass than my conversation, for he paid scant attention and, after nuzzling me for a moment, started to graze again. I went back to my seat on the gate and stayed there until the stillness of the morning was broken by the peals of Fledgewood Church's bells, calling its people to early service. Then I knew that it was nearly breakfast time and I walked back along the garden path to the house. In the hall, I met Jill.

"Gosh! Did you really get the pony in the field for fifteen guineas?" she said.

"Yes. Isn't he a bargain?" I said gaily.

"A *bargain*—you *are* hopeful—you wouldn't see a pony like that in the market, unless there was something very wrong with it. Are you sure he is not a confirmed rearer or bolter?"

"Yes, certain," I replied happily. "I rode him back from Dilford in a halter and he went beautifully."

"Probably he was doped," said Jill.

At that moment Barbara came down the stairs.

"Hullo, Augusta!" she said. "I've seen your pony out of the window. How on earth do you think you will be able to manage a well-bred animal like that? He will need quieter handling than that Shetland, you know."

"I bet he jibs," said Jill.

"He doesn't," I said.

The gong rang and we went into the dining-room. A few minutes later Aunt Margaret joined us, and served the bacon and eggs. She did not mention Daybreak.

I was terribly hungry and I gobbled my food, and upset my milk, and this annoyed Aunt Margaret, who told me off and rang for Susan to mop it up. Towards the end of the meal the conversation turned to High Jinks, who was arriving by horse-box the following Thursday. Jill told me that he had won twenty-nine firsts for jumping, during the last show season, and added that she was going to beat that score this year.

After breakfast, Barbara, Jill, and I went to see

70

Daybreak. I put a halter on and held him, while my cousins ran their hands down his legs and looked at his teeth. Then I led him round the field at the walk and trot, every now and then turning him sharply in different directions, while they watched to see that he was quite sound on all his legs. At last they finished and Jill said, "One thing's definite—that pony *must* be vicious."

"Yes," said Barbara. "You've made a bad mistake and wasted fifteen guineas, I'm afraid."

"He wouldn't be sold at Dilford Market for a sum like that, unless there was something funny about him, that's certain," said Jill. "Of course, it's your own fault," she went on. "Why didn't you ask our advice? We could have told you not to try the market—it's the last place for some one who knows nothing about ponies to try—you're simply bound to be done."

"Oh, shut up," I said.

"There you are. You see, it's no use, Jill; she doesn't want to learn. Come on; let's go indoors," said Barbara.

They went away and I patted and talked to Daybreak, and told him how beastly they were. Then I heard Aunt Margaret calling me. She was in the garden and, when I reached her, she told me that, although I was a very naughty little girl, to buy a pony without telling her, she had decided that my faults were mostly due to wrong upbringing and that I could keep Daybreak, so long as I could control him. She added that I must look after him entirely myself and that he must live out all the year round. Then she asked whether I had written to thank Captain Houseman for the money and, when she heard that I had not, she said that I must write directly after lunch. "Now," she finished up, "you had better change for

71

church, and don't forget to put on that nice hat I bought you."

I know that I should have told her about that *nice hat's* fate then, but somehow I could not; I thanked her, because it sounded polite and she had told me that I could keep Daybreak, and slowly went upstairs to my bedroom. I changed into a skirt and the coat which I had worn at the market—putting safety pins where the buttons had been. Then I sat on my bed and tried to think of the most tactful way to explain to Aunt Margaraet how much I had needed fifteen shillings. I knew that she would be furious and I suppose that really I was frightened, but there was no way out—she had to be told. When, a little later, I heard her asking Jill whether she had remembered her prayer book, I left my bedroom and went down and found her and my cousins in the drawing-room. They were standing with their backs to me, a fair, bobbed head each side of Aunt Margaret's greying one, the hair of which was strictly forced into a single roll. How formidable they looked!

"I say," I said. "I haven't got a hat. I've sold the one you bought me. I'm awfully sorry."

Aunt Margaret swung round. "How dare you?" she said.

"I'm sorry, but you see, I made a mistake and thought that I had bought Daybreak for pounds—really it was guineas," I said.

"Words fail me, Augusta, I wouldn't have believed any one could be so ungrateful," said Aunt Margaret; "but, of course, I can see you are deliberately trying to avoid going to church."

"That's not true," I said angrily. "I don't mind going to church in the least. Anyway, the hat was mine, after you gave it to me, and so I thought that

72

I could do as I liked with it; and now that it has saved me from complete disaster and helped me buy a pony, I am more grateful to you for giving it to me than ever before. Can't I borrow Barbara's handkerchief again," I went on. "It looked all right last time."

"Certainly not," said Aunt Margaret, shaking with anger. "I'm not going to be made to look a fool again. While we are at church, you will sit down in the nursery and write: *I am a naughty, deceitful, disobedient, ungrateful little girl,* out five hundred times."

"O.K.," I said, feeling very dismal because the day was sunny and spring-like, and it seemed a pity to waste a beautiful morning sitting stuffily indoors, writing the same useless sentence again and again. I would have felt better if she had set me some manual task, like sweeping up leaves or weeding, or even hoeing or digging; for though they might have made my back ache, I would at least have had the comfort of knowing that I had saved some one a little trouble, and done a little good.

"If you don't write properly and tidily, you will have to do it over again," Aunt Margaret threatened as I walked slowly upstairs to the nursery. On my way, I paused and looked out of the passage window, from which you can see the ponies' field. Curtis had just turned Sandy out and he and Daybreak were galloping round with their tails kinked up over their backs. They looked lovely and I thought that they were very lucky to be able to gallop and play in the sparkling sunshine, and not bother about gratefulness and hats.

Once in the nursery, I tried to start my monotonous work, but fate seemed against me. To begin with, I could not find any paper and, annoyingly enough, it was in its place all the time, only I passed it over twice, purely because I was thinking about Daybreak instead of searching carefully. Then I could not remember how to spell *naughty, deceitful, disobedient* or *ungrateful*, and I had to look them up in the dictionary, because I thought that Aunt Margaret might make me write all the sentences again, if I made mistakes in spelling—that took ages. Finally, I could not stop myself thinking about Daybreak and whenever he was in my mind, I dropped a blot or my lines became crooked and my words slanting. It was exasperating, but in spite of these mishaps time passed incredibly quickly and I had only written the sentence four hundred and twenty-nine times, when my cousins arrived home after church.

They came running up the stairs, shouting my name, and dashed into the nursery.

"Well," said Jill. "I *was* right; you *have* been done."

"He's a gelding too, so you can't keep him for breeding," said Barbara.

"What has happened?" I asked, my heart pounding furiously.

"If only you had asked our advice, the circumstances would have been very different," said Barbara.

"He's dead lame, and I should say it's incurable," said Jill. "I knew he must be vicious or unsound as soon as I saw him," she went on. "No pony like him would be sold at the market unless it had something very wrong with it."

"I'm sorry for you; but, you know, when inexperienced people like you start buying ponies on their own, they are bound to be caught out," said Barbara, with her slow, superior smile.

"For goodness' sake, shut up," I said. "I am going to see him."

As I ran down the garden path, a moment later, I cherished a wild hope that my cousins might have made a mistake, that Daybreak was sound after all; but once in the field this was shattered; I saw the terrible truth with my own eyes and knew that my cousins had not lied. He was walking round after Sandy, slowly, painfully, dragging a hind leg with the toe resting on the ground. He looked hopelessly and permanently crippled and frightfully pathetic and with a loud babyish roar, I burst into tears.

My perfect pony was dead lame.

My cousins were close behind me, and I heard Jill say "I told you so." Whether she was speaking to me or Barbara I did not know, nor did I care. All that mattered to me was that the beautiful, perfect pony, which I had bought with such difficulty, was dead lame, crippled, miserable.

"I am afraid he will have to be destroyed," said Jill,

raising her voice. "They are bound to have tried every possible cure before sending him down to the market."

"The knacker might give you a pound or two for his body, but I'm afraid you'll have to count the rest of your money as a dead loss," said Barbara.

"It's a terrible pity," said Jill, "because he's a really useful sort, although not quite your type. Look at his long sloping shoulder and short back, and his fine head."

Suddenly I could bear their talk no longer; something inside me seemed to snap; I lost control of my temper.

"Go away," I shouted. "Leave me alone. He won't be destroyed, never, never, never. I shall keep him always. He's mine, not yours—you interfering beasts."

"Really," said Barbara, "you must keep calm, Augusta. We all know it is very disappointing for you, but it's no good shouting—after all, you have only yourself to blame."

Angry though I was, those words made me realise for the first time how much Barbara resembled her mother—*you have only yourself to blame*—Aunt Margaret had said that when they killed Matilda, poor Matilda.

"I hate you," I said.

"It's lunch-time," remarked Jill.

"I'm going to ring up the vet," said Barbara. "It's cruel to leave that wretched pony dragging his leg around—the sooner he's out of his misery the better."

I did not speak. What was there to say? My temper had gone; soon my cousins left me and I stood and watched poor, good Daybreak dragging round after Sandy and wished that he would stop and stand still. His slow, painful progress made me feel sick, because

76

I thought that his crippled leg must be hurting terribly, and in a very few minutes I was crying again. I was still crying when Aunt Margaret came to fetch me in for lunch.

"Now, dear," she said. "There's no point in being silly and crying. Come indoors and have something to eat. The vet will be here soon." She spoke in the calming voice one might use to a person who was on the verge of a nervous breakdown.

I followed her indoors without a word and ate most of my lunch, although I was not hungry. My cousins talked tactfully about the weather and food.

After lunch, Aunt Margaret made Barbara, Jill and me sit on the lawn and wait and watch for the vet. We must have stayed there for more than half an hour, but not one of us spoke. I believe that my cousins thought I was better left alone, that I might start throwing things—you never knew with queer people.

At last a long, black car came up the drive and stopped outside the house. A fat, fair man, wearing a camel hair coat and homburg hat, stepped out and knocked at the front door.

"That's the vet," said Jill.

We all rose and walked solemnly to the car to find Aunt Margaret already there, explaining about Day-break.

"He drags his leg after him," she was saying, "and, of course, he *did* come from the market."

"Can I see him?" said the vet; and by his tone I guessed that he did not like the Fielding family.

Aunt Margaret led the way to the field, and my heart bumped noisily, against my ribs, as I followed —last of every one. Daybreak was standing still in a corner and Barbara pointed him out.

"He's a good-looking pony," said the vet.

77

"Unfortunately, 'handsome is what handsome does,'" said Jill.

We all walked across the field abreast and, when we had almost reached Daybreak, he moved off. For a moment, I could not believe my eyes—he wasn't dragging his leg—he was sound.

"Oh!" I said, and my heart seemed to leap with joy.

The vet laughed. "I don't think I shall need my humane killer to-day," he said.

"When my daughter rang you up, he was dead lame, dragging his hind leg, as though it was broken," said Aunt Margaret defensively.

"Can you put a halter on him, please?" said the vet. "You say he dragged his leg," he went on. "I suppose with his toe resting on the ground. Has he had a chance to come down to-day? Perhaps he's been galloping on his own."

"Yes, he has," I said, my hopes rising as swiftly as the smoke had risen from the burning ricks, over a week ago. "I saw him this morning, out of the window, simply tearing round with Sandy."

By now I had put Sunshine's halter on Daybreak, and the vet stooped and ran his hand down his near hind leg. Then he stood up, and said:

"He must have partially dislocated the patella, while galloping round this morning. Now it is back in position again and so he is quite sound. I don't think it will happen again—it's not as though he's young or in very low condition—but give him a day or two's rest, and let me know if it does."

He patted Daybreak, and I took off the halter. "I am sorry you had a journey for nothing," I said.

"Not at all, not at all; it was a pleasure. And how are the other ponies?" said the vet.

As we walked back to the car, Aunt Margaret told

him about Topper and High Jinks, and all the time I felt like shouting with joy. Then, after we had thanked him for coming, the vet drove away down the drive in the long, purring car and I turned, and singing the "Isle of Capri" at the top of my voice, I ran back to the field and Daybreak.

Much later in the day, I remembered the incompleted five hundred sentences.

CHAPTER SIX

Two days passed before I rode Daybreak, and I spent them at Bellaughton, the most fashionable girl's school in Dilford. Although I do not like schools at all, I remember that at the time I was pleased to have children, other than my cousins, to talk with, and because all was new to me, it was more interesting than might be expected. My cousins went there too, and I found that although they were thought *bumptious* by some of the older girls, they were very popular because they both excelled at games and Jill was captain of the junior tennis and netball teams.

The third day was Wednesday and on Wednesdays Bellaughton's day girls leave an hour earlier than on the other week days, so I decided to seize the opportunity to try Daybreak. On the way home in the car, Jill kindly said that I could borrow Sunshine's saddle, but not her bridle, because my hands were too heavy to use a double bridle and Sunshine does not possess a snaffle. Then Barbara offered to lend me Sweep's which is a plain jointed one. I thanked them both, and wondered whether their sudden change of heart was

I caught Daybreak.

due to the gnawing pangs of remorse or merely curiosity to know whether Daybreak was vicious, as soon as possible.

When we arrived home, I dashed upstairs and changed out of my beastly gym tunic—it was one which Jill had outgrown—and tore round to the ponies' field. I took some of my cousins' oats from the forage room and caught Daybreak, and tied Sandy to the gate so that he would not get in the way. I borrowed Sunshine's brush and groomed Daybreak's already shiny coat. While I worked, I whistled and sang gay songs, and laughed when I thought of my cousins imagining that my pony was a bolter or rearer.

"We'll show them, won't we?" I said to him, and he cocked back an ear and listened.

"They think you're vicious," I went on; "but they'll get a surprise when they find you have perfect manners, won't they?"

I felt sure that Daybreak would go well. After all, I had cantered him in a halter, and there was no reason to suppose that he would not be equally good to-day.

When I had finished grooming, I put on the saddle and bridle, and Curtis saw me and was very disagreeable. He told me that he had just cleaned the tack and put it away for the night. I offered to clean it again when I had finished riding, but he only muttered and grumbled, so I took no more notice.

I was mounting, when Aunt Margaret and my cousins arrived on the scene.

"Wait a moment," said Jill. "That bit is too low—a snaffle should be as high in the mouth as is possible without wrinkling the lips." She pulled it up a hole and looked at the noseband and throatlash and saw that they were not too tight. Then I mounted, with the same, awful feeling in the pit of my stomach as when

I walked into the drawing-room to tell all three days before. . . . Supposing his patella slips again and the vet says it is incurable. What shall I do then, I wondered.

Barbara was holding Daybreak's head.

"Honestly, Augusta, I should like to know what you propose to do if he *is* a rearer or bolter?" she said, and again she smiled in her quiet, superior way.

"Cure him," I said, for there was no other answer, since I would not sell him.

"Gosh!" said Jill. "Aren't we getting clever?"

"Considering you can't manage a ten-hand, Shetland pony yet, I hardly think you can cure a confirmed bolter or rearer of fourteen two," said Barbara.

"Don't let's bother about a hypothesis. Please leave go of his head," I said, and I was hot with anger, although I had the consolation of knowing that my cousins were temporarily snubbed, because neither knew the meaning of the word, *hypothesis*.

Barbara let go of Daybreak's head and I squeezed him with my legs, and away we went. The sick feeling within me disappeared. Now we will show them, I thought.

Then, suddenly, Daybreak started to shake his head —up and down, from side to side—almost as though he was mad.

"Stop it," I said, and my heart beat furiously, and my mind filled at once with dismal thoughts. . . . Supposing he was a runaway—supposing he was insane.

"Trot on," I said, and squeezed with my calves. He broke into the same lovely trot that I admired so much, coming back from Dilford; but only for a second could I enjoy the smooth, rhythmical strides before all was marred by violent, crazy head shaking.

82

"Don't, don't," I said, and I sent him into a canter, but still he went on—shake, shake, shake—incessantly, incurably.

I looked at my aunt and cousins standing by the gate—triumphant; glad that I had had a lesson—and I felt hot tears pricking behind my eyes; soon they overflowed and coursed down my cheeks and fell in confusion upon the saddle. . . . Why do I cry so easily, I wondered. Then I remembered the significant and unfinished piece of advice: *I shouldn't buy that grey, miss, he's* . . . What could the end have been? Mad, perhaps.

"Stop shaking, please, Daybreak," I said, and I pulled him up to a walk and dropped the reins on to his neck, but still he shook his head. So my cousins were right, I thought; they knew that he must be vicious or unsound, but I was too pleased with myself to listen to them. I only told them to shut up. No wonder they think I am conceited. No wonder they think I am queer. No wonder they despise me.

"Augusta," shouted Aunt Margaret from the gate. "Come here."

I picked up the reins and turned Daybreak, and we walked across to her. She told me simply to dismount because my pony was dangerous, and she did not want an accident.

"We think he has a tumour on the brain," said Jill.

"O.K.," I said, and, looking away from my cousins so that they would not see that I was crying, I dismounted on the right-hand side.

"Wrong side, Augusta," said Jill.

"Shut up. I know," I said and straight away I regretted my snubbing retort. I knew that I had sounded frightfully conceited. But I did not feel like making amends. I took off the tack in sulky silence; still with my face turned away from my cousins.

Soon Barbara spoke. "I am sorry you have had such a nasty surprise, Augusta," she said, and I believed she really meant it.

"Yes, Augusta," said Aunt Margaret, "that is what comes of being deceitful and disobedient. Think what else you could have bought for fifteen pounds."

I wanted to be very rude then. I wanted to be cold, scornful, squashing; to tell them that I would not exchange Daybreak for anything else in the world; yet I could not trust my voice; I had to remain silent. They thought that I was subdued. I believe Aunt Margaret even thought that I was repentant. Her voice took on a kinder tone when she spoke again.

"Put the saddle and bridle in the tack-room, dear, and then come in and have some tea," she said.

"There's honey to-day," added Barbara.

My cousins talked about High Jinks during tea, and I spoke very little. As soon as we had finished eating, I ran, unseen, to the field. I caught Daybreak and put a halter on him; then, with a fast-beating heart, I mounted him from off the gate. I squeezed him with my calves; he walked and, to my surprise, he did not shake his head; not even when, a few minutes later, I trotted and cantered. I felt very relieved and very pleased. But somehow I could not whistle, I could only pat him and say silly things like, "Clever Daybreak; darling Daybreak," and for some reason I spoke in a whisper.

I rode him in a halter for about ten minutes and then I put Sweep's pelham on instead. Straight away, he started to shake his head up and down, from side to side.

"Oh, Daybreak, for goodness' sake don't," I said. I

took off the bridle and looked in his mouth in case it was sore. Inside it was pink with a brownish tinge, and there was no sound of soreness. I felt sure that Daybreak hadn't a tumour on the brain, and I tried him in all the bridles I could find, but in every one it was the same—shake, shake, shake.

"What is it, my poor fellow?" I asked, and I wished that he could answer. At last I gave up and turned him loose. Then I fetched a bucket of hot water from the kitchen. I started to collect together the bridles and Curtis appeared and was furious when he saw all the tack that I had dirtied.

"I don't know what's the good of my cleaning those bridles, when you dirties them directly. I shall tell Madam of you, that I shall," he said.

"But I'll clean them again, now," I said.

"And a good clean that'll be, too," he said sarcastically.

I opened my mouth to speak, but by then he was giving vent to his anger by banging buckets about in the forage-room, and all other noise was drowned.

Whistling, I started to clean the bridles in the tack-room. A few minutes later, Jill came in and said that I was putting on the saddle soap with too wet a rag and using too hot water.

"You should never make the soap lather and hot water ruins leather; and for *goodness' sake* leave my saddle for Curtis. I don't want it spoilt as well as the bridles," she said. "By the way," she went on, "I said you were *not* to borrow Sunshine's bridle. I think you might do as I ask occasionally, instead of *always* behaving as though the whole place belonged to you."

"I only put it on and took it off again; that won't have hurt it," I said, beginning to whistle again.

"And what about your wonderful cleaning with hot

85

I started to clean the bridles.

water? I suppose that won't have hurt it either," said Jill spitefully.

"Actually," I said, "it wasn't so very hot, and look. I don't think it's done it any harm." I glanced at the bridle, as I spoke, and I could not see that it was any the worse for my clean.

Jill changed the subject. "What have you been doing? Not riding Daybreak, I hope."

"Yes," I said gaily. "I have, and in a halter he doesn't shake his head at all, so I don't think he *has* a tumour on the brain."

"A fat lot you know about it," said Jill; "and, by the way, if you must ride that crazy animal, let me advise you not to use a double bridle. You are not gifted with light hands and unless you're careful, you'll have that pony 'behind the bit' in no time."

"I only rode him for a second on the top rein," I said, and I began to whistle, "To-day I feel so happy."

Jill walked about the tack-room, idly picking things up only to put them down again a few seconds later. I could see that my whistling annoyed her, because she loudly sighed, but I did not stop, instead I changed to another tune, "The Isle of Capri." At last she could bear it no longer.

"For goodness' sake, stop that awful row; it's enough to give any one a headache for life," she said.

"Sorry," I said. "I didn't know you were a victim of nerves."

"I'm not," she snapped angrily. "You drive us all mad—either you are whistling and singing the house down or moping about looking like a sick worm. Why can't you behave like a normal person?"

"Oh, do shut up. I'll throw something at you in a minute," I said.

"Now, now, don't get into a petty temper. It's quite true," said Jill.

"Oh, *do* go away; I was getting on beautifully without you," I said, and it was all I could do to stop myself throwing the saddle soap at her. I felt furious. The thought that I might look like a sick worm was particularly annoying, especially as I knew that I was often gloomy—more so than most children.

Jill said, "Yes, ruining all the tack. Why can't you leave it for Curtis?"

I did not answer, and after sighing a few times, Jill walked from the tack-room. Then I hurried because I knew the time must be late. Somehow, I had finished when the gong rang for dinner.

During this meal no one mentioned Daybreak, but I heard that Sandy was to live in the field with him, and that High Jinks was to occupy Sandy's box, while a new one was built. I tried to join in the conversation, because of not seeming like a sick worm; but, after being corrected twice for interrupting and once for going off the point, I gave up in despair.

After dinner I spent an hour over my preparation, and then went to bed with a book on horsemanship.

When we arrived home from school the following afternoon, we found High Jinks in Sandy's loose-box. He was a lightly built chestnut pony with two white socks and a long mane and tail, and he looked fiery, and dashing, and expensive. While we gazed at him, he tore round the box and neighed excitedly.

"He's showy, isn't he?" said Jill. "And just look at his hocks—absolutely correct for a jumper."

I said, "He's got a nice shoulder and I like his colour, and——"

"*Nice*. A shoulder can't be *nice*—long and sloping, perhaps, but *not nice*, that's only suitable for things

88

like sweets and cakes," interrupted Jill. "And as for his colour," she went on, "let me tell you, 'a good horse is *never* a bad colour.'"

"I think it's time for tea," said Barbara. "And Mummy says you can jump him after tea and not bother about doing all your prep."

"Good," said Jill. "Curtis, bring out some of the show jumps; I am going to ride the new chestnut after tea. I shan't want anything under three feet six," she shouted grandly.

We went indoors and I felt glad that I was looking after Daybreak myself. I realised how little Jill would know about her pony's character, how much she would miss. High Jinks would never whinny when he saw her or listen for her footsteps in the early morning. He would prefer Curtis, the man who fed him and looked after him when he was ill or tired or lame.

"Now for the great event," said Jill, as we walked to the field after tea. We found High Jinks saddled and bridled and I was surprised to see that he was wearing a tight, running martingale and a hood. Jill saw me eyeing them critically. "He's got proper show jumping tackle," she said.

"Is he difficult to control?" I asked.

"No, just high spirited; like all the best jumpers, he's full of 'pep,'" Jill replied, and she led the pony out of the box and mounted.

Once she was on I could see that High Jinks was a handful. He pranced and jogged, instead of walking as he was told, and every now and then he snorted. Jill tried to make him go more quietly, but in vain, and after a few minutes she gave up and trotted and cantered.

"He's a grand mover," commented Aunt Margaret; and I noticed that he carried his ugly head exceptionally high.

"I'm going to jump him now," shouted Jill, and she turned High Jinks and rode at a white gate of three feet six inches in height. He approached slowly, and then as he reached the wings he shot faster and cleared it with a flourish.

"Bravo, Jill!" shouted Aunt Margaret.

"Well done," said Barbara.

"That was super," said Jill. "Now, I'm going over the wall and triple."

Those two jumps High Jinks cleared in the same dashing style, as he had taken the gate. Then Jill shouted to Curtis, who had just come from his tea, and told him to raise all three jumps, to four feet. This done, she shouted to us that we were now about to see some super jumping. She turned High Jinks and they cleared the gate, the wall and the triple in perfect time with one another. Then I felt jealous because I could not ride so well, and instead of politely congratulating her like every one else, I remained sulkily silent. I know this was horrible of me, and later in bed I cursed myself for being a beast; but at the time I could not stop it.

After Jill had been praised for a long five minutes, she said that she must go over the jumps at four feet six before she stopped riding, and again she ordered Curtis to raise them. Then, with a conceited smile, she accomplished the feat once more—she cleared them all.

"Darling! That was wonderful; your riding was brilliant," said Aunt Margaret.

"The timing was perfect," added Barbara.

"I gave him the aid to increase at exactly the right

moment, didn't I, Mummy?" said Jill, and her eyes were shining with happiness.

"Yes, you were splendid, my pet," replied Aunt Margaret.

"One thing is definite—John Dunlop and Susan Phillips won't stand a chance against you," remarked Barbara.

"We will have to think of where we can put all your new cups; you've nearly overflowed the dining-room," said Aunt Margaret.

"I'll put them in the drawing-room, where they will be seen," Jill told us, dismounting.

Curtis took High Jinks, who was lathered with sweat, and led him into the vacant loose-box.

"Now, children, you must come in and do your prep," said Aunt Margaret .

I had hoped to ride Daybreak, but I saw that this was out of the question and so, dismal with jealousy, I followed my cousins indoors.

When, much later in the evening, I went to bed I felt strangely gloomy and I hated myself for it, because now that I owned a pony I expected to be always happy. In spite of the gloomy feeling, I slept well and wakened early in a good temper. I looked out of my window and saw, beyond a line of dark young firs, a blood-red sun climbing the eastern sky.
. . . What a lovely morning for a ride, I thought, and I jumped out of bed and dressed and washed quickly. I was in the field by about seven o'clock. I caught Daybreak easily. "Now for some experiments," I said, and put Sunshine's saddle on him. Then, after taking the noseband off, I put on Sweep's bridle and mounted.

I was doomed to disappointment—straight away he shook the head which I admired so much, up and

Before catching Daybreak.

down, from side to side. I dismounted at once, feeling exasperated beyond measure; with a curse, I undid some stud billets and took off the bit. I put the nose-band on again and joined the reins to it. Then I mounted, only to find that the head shaking went on, just the same, bit or no bit.

"Oh, Daybreak, why must you do it; why, why, why?" I said, and I was near crying. Of course, he could not reply, and instead he shook his head all the harder—or so it seemed to me. . . . What can I take off the bridle now? I thought; and then I knew—the brow-band. I dismounted. "This is our last hope, Day-break," I said.

My hands shaking with excitement, I fixed on the bit again and removed the brow-band. Then, with a queer, grim feeling which was new to me, I mounted for the third time that spring morning. I squeezed my pony's sides with my calves and he walked, taking long, swinging strides, and for a moment he shook his head; then, suddenly, he stopped—he stopped shaking. I sat very still; I said nothing. I waited for him to start again, with a fast-beating heart. Time passed and every minute I felt happier and safer. Soon we trotted and later we cantered, and still all was well. "Day-break, you are wonderful, marvellous," I said, and then I started to whistle.

Soon Curtis appeared, and I knew by his face that he was annoyed with me—probably because I had dirtied some tack and left a brow-band hanging on the gate.

"Good-morning," I said, and he did not answer, but went into the forage-room, while Sweep and Sunshine called to him with soft whinnies, their eyes shining. Now, I knew by the empty feeling in my tummy that it was breakfast time and I dismounted, and patted my pony for a long while, before finally turning him loose. "To-morrow, if I wake up early we will go for a hack," I told him, and he did not listen, but walked away to roll in the luscious, spring grass.

CHAPTER SEVEN

ON Friday I rose very early in the morning and, again, I rushed to the field, as soon as I had washed and dressed; but on this occasion the countryside was wrapped in darkness, for the time was half-past four.

Luckily, I had no difficulty in finding Daybreak, because he was standing by the gate and he tactfully whinnied when he heard my footsteps. I gave him a piece of toast—I had saved it from dinner the night before—and feeling my way carefully with one hand I led him to the tack-room. I switched on the light and fetched a halter. Then I groomed and saddled and bridled him in the doorway, taking great care to remember to take off the brow-band. I did not waste any time over this and I was feeling rather pleased with myself when, only a few minutes later, we walked down the back drive into the road.

The air was warm; the first eerie streak of light stole across the eastern sky. For a brief moment, but for the clip, clop of Daybreak's hoofs, the world around me slumbered; then the stillness of early morning was shattered; a dog barked, and a train hooted a long, long way away. Only a few seconds later the air was filled with the shrill clarion of a thousand cocks. Dawn was here; grey and secretive, lurking behind a veil of mist—this spring morning.

Why don't I always get up so early?

Before me stretched the road and I felt happy, because Daybreak walked quickly without shaking his head and all my worst troubles seemed over. I made plans for the rosy future, for gymkhanas, for hunting. Only one thing worried me—the tack. I could not always borrow my cousins' and, although I did not mind riding bareback, I thought of the horse shows and of how ridiculous I would look entering for a jumping class in a halter. But I was in a cheerful mood and I soon reminded myself that my birthday was in less than three weeks and that some one was certain to give me a saddle or bridle.

"We'll get fixed up somehow," I said to Daybreak, and I started to whistle "The Skye Boat Song." Far away to the left a cow moo-ed and a man shouted; somewhere a donkey brayed and a horse answered. . . . Why don't I always get up so early? I wondered and I patted my pony's sleek, grey neck.

A little later, we turned into the vast beech woods behind Longdrop. Here the birds were singing with all the ardour of spring and Daybreak's hoofs made little noise, for the ground was still carpeted with last autumn's red-brown leaves.

It was heavenly to be riding my pony with only the quiet dignity of the trees for company—with no spying cousins nearby to warn and criticise. Broad, winding cart tracks led away from us in all directions, but I chose to take the one which I had walked along with Aunt Margaret on a Sunday afternoon, several weeks before. I was afraid that exploring might make me late for breakfast, and for once my fears were justified. The track which I chose ran round the edge of the smallest of the woods and, here and there, the ground was so soft and free of roots that we could canter. Daybreak seemed fresh, and pretended to see bogeys, and shied at ridiculous things like stumps and puddles.

Time passed quickly and, as we turned for home, the sun broke through the swaying boughs of the beech-trees and made crazy, dancing patterns amongst their shabby trunks. Later, when I reached the Fledgewood road, I met postmen and milkmen on

Riding through the beechwood.

their early rounds, and passed houses with drawn curtains. As I went by one glaring, modern villa, I heard an alarm clock efficiently screeching, and I imagined its owner turning over and cursing at the thought of morning and work. Then I heard a church clock strike eight and suddenly I realised that this was

97

D

breakfast time and that, unless I hurried, I would be late for school.

In spite of the road being hard and slippery, I sent Daybreak into a trot, for I thought of Aunt Margaret wondering what had become of me, and I knew that she would be very angry. The road seemed far, far longer than I had imagined, and soon Daybreak was hot, and I pulled him up to a walk, and was haunted by remorse, because I had thought of myself before my pony. Hours seemed to have passed, when we reached the main Dilford road, which you have to cross to get from Fledgewood to Tree Tops. I was in the middle of crossing when a black car entered it from the other side; inside the car was Aunt Margaret, and Barbara and Jill were there too, with gym tunics and satchels—all ready for school. I longed to gallop away, to hide in the beech woods, but I pulled up Daybreak and waited, because I did not want to be thought a coward.

Aunt Margaret stopped the car and opened the window. "Augusta, how dare you behave like this?" she asked and, even though she was very angry, her voice was under perfect control.

"I'm sorry," I said.

"*Sorry*. That's what you always say, but you still go on disobeying my orders, deceiving, lying," said Aunt Margaret.

"Who gave you permission to borrow Sunshine's saddle?" asked Jill.

"No one," I replied.

Aunt Margaret said: "Augusta, your behaviour is disgraceful and if you think you are going to avoid school this way, you are very highly mistaken. I am going to take Jill and Barbara there now, and if you are not ready waiting with your satchel and books by the time I get back, I'll sell your tiresome pony; goodness knows he's been nothing but a nuisance since you bought him."

"O.K. I'll hurry," I said, and I finished crossing the Dilford road and trotted down the one that leads from it to Tree Tops.

Once home, I gave Daybreak a handful of my cousins' oats and plonked the saddle and bridle in the tack-room. Then I tore indoors and upstairs to my bedroom. I changed quickly, just dragging on my blouse, which I had left buttoned up the night before, and shoving my feet into laced-up shoes. I thought that I had been efficient and brisk for once but, when leaving my room, I glanced in the looking-glass. I saw that my tunic had no belt and my blouse was inside out. I cursed and undressed and put my blouse on the right way in, nearly tearing off the collar in my haste. Then I frantically searched for my tunic belt, every moment expecting to hear the car turn up the drive. I pulled out and upset drawers, opened and slammed shut cupboards, dragged all the blankets off my bed and moved most of the furniture, but all in vain; I did not find the belt. I thought of Daybreak being sold and I gave a loud wail of despair. Betty came running up the stairs.

"What ever on earth's the matter?" she asked.

"Oh, quick! Please," I said. "I've lost my belt, please, have you seen it?"

Betty walked into my bedroom and gasped at the sight of it. Clothes, blankets, drawers, eiderdowns and books were strewn all over the floor in one ghastly muddle.

"You naughty girl," she said. "Nobody would think I had just done this room, that they wouldn't." Now

99

you put all those drawers back at once and make your bed. I'm not going to do it again—that I'm not."

"Sorry, I will," I said, starting to chuck my clothes back into the drawers. "But, please, Betty, the belt—where is it?"

"All right; I'm getting it. Any one would think I was a machine. I've a good mind not to help you, that I have," replied Betty, opening my wardrobe and fetching the belt from within.

"I hung it up with your ties," she told me.

"Oh, thank you; thanks terribly," I said, buttoning it round my waist and dashing from the room.

"Come back, you naughty girl; you haven't made your bed or shut the drawers," shouted Betty, "and I'm not going to do it, that I'm not."

"All right," I said and, turning round, I retraced my footsteps. I made my bed quickly—just dragging it together—and, leaving the drawers, tore to the nursery to fetch my satchel. But Fate was against me that morning, and I could not find it anywhere. I gave another wail of despair and Betty came again and asked what was the matter *this* time. I told her, and she was awfully nice. She helped me search and kept very calm, which was a good thing, because I was becoming quite hysterical. I hurried terribly and every few minutes I knocked something over or tripped and fell. All the time I was thinking about Daybreak being sold and I frequently said: "Oh, where can it be, where can it be? I shall be too late."

"Where you put it, there it'll be," Betty invariably replied. At last she found it under the sofa. How it came there I can't imagine. Only a few seconds afterwards, we heard the car turn up the drive and Aunt Margaret hooting the horn. Thanking Betty for the

100

third time, I dashed downstairs, through the hall and into the car.

All the way to Bellaughton Aunt Margaret lectured me on my bad behaviour and she told me that I was never again to ride Daybreak before breakfast, not even in the field. When I arrived at school I was feeling sunk in gloom. Later, during lessons, I could not keep my attention from wandering and I made hundreds of careless mistakes, and was made to "stay in" during break as a punishment. Even in the evening my preparation seemed twice as long as usual, and I only had time to speak to Daybreak for a very few minutes, before going to bed.

The next day was Saturday, so there was no school. At breakfast, my cousins decided to go for a hack in the morning on Sweep and Sunshine, and Jill said that she would jump High Jinks in the afternoon. I wanted to give Daybreak a jumping lesson, but I did not wish my cousins to watch, so I decided to ride bareback in the morning—High Jink's saddle would not fit Daybreak. No one asked me what I was going to do. I think that Aunt Margaret and Jill had decided that to ignore Daybreak was the best way of showing their contempt and disapproval.

I saved some toast crust at breakfast and waited until my cousins had started for their hack, before catching Daybreak. Curtis was in the field preparing a course of jumps for Jill and High Jinks to practise over in the afternoon. They all looked very formidable and I knew they were too high for Daybreak and me at the moment. I tied my pony up and searched for a bar for us to jump. Although I looked for ages, I could not find anything which was at all suitable. At last, in exasperation, I fetched three deck-chairs from the garage and, leaving them shut up, leaned them against some buckets. This made a long, tempting jump of about two feet six inches in height and I mounted Daybreak from the gate. Curtis said nothing and I thought that he looked disagreeable, but a little later, when Sandy was in my way, he kindly caught him and put him in Sweep's loose-box.

I schooled Daybreak in half the field for about a quarter of an hour, mostly at the walk and canter because they were more comfortable bareback than the trot. Then, with a loud-beating heart, I rode him towards the jump. I had read in several of my cousins' books on horsemanship, that the rider should make his horse increase his speed during the last three strides of the "approach" to a jump. I remembered this and I gave Daybreak a little kick at what I thought was the right moment. He seemed to lengthen his stride and I hoped that he was going over and I leaned forward and held on to the mane. The next second I was whizzing through the air and the ground was coming to meet me. It came nearer and nearer and then with a soft thud we met. I landed on my head, but I did not hurt myself. I leaped to my feet and there was Daybreak calmly looking at me with pricked ears, from the other side of the jump.

"You bad fellow, refusing," I said, and I lowered the deck-chairs by leaning them a little more. Then I mounted and once more we cantered towards the jump. This time, I was prepared for the worst and I did not come off when he again refused dead.

"Oh, dear," I said, and I looked round to see whether any one had seen my feeble riding. Curtis had gone, but upstairs, looking out of the passage window was Aunt Margaret, stern and disapproving. She moved away when she noticed that I had seen her, and I thought that she was coming to tell me that I shouldn't have taken the deck-chairs. I hoped she wasn't, but, as they were too high, anyway, I tied

Daybreak to the field-gate and put them back in the garage. Then I went to the tool-shed and fetched two brooms and a hoe. I rested them in a line on the buckets and then I mounted Daybreak and, to my surprise, he jumped it beautifully, without hesitation. I patted him for ages and fed him with toast crust. Then we jumped it once the other way and stopped. I turned him loose and only just in time. A few minutes later my cousins came back from their ride. They saw my jump and Jill pointed out that hoes are dangerous because they are sharp, and Barbara said that if I had waited until the afternoon I could have borrowed Sweep's tack. Then Curtis appeared and took their ponies and we all went in to wash for lunch.

In the afternoon High Jinks jumped two clear rounds over a course of four feet high jumps. Aunt Margaret said that he was grand, and Barbara that he was perfect, and Jill wrote to Stephen and told him to look out for her photograph in the papers. For the rest of the day they planned the future, and it was decided that the Stokely Show would be the first in which these budding champions would compete. It is a large and well-known, three-day provincial show and was being held in twenty-three days' time—when Jill and High Jinks would be completely used to one another. I secretly wished that I could take Daybreak and enter too, but I knew that I could not ride nearly well enough, and I told myself that I must wait until the Dilford Show, which is always held on August Bank Holiday.

I am not going to attempt to describe the next sixteen days, because nothing at all exciting happened. I rode Daybreak six times and gave him four jumping lessons, each time borrowing a decayed broom and an old mop from Betty. Nearly always I rode bareback but I only fell off once, and that was when we were

103

trotting and Daybreak swerved. By the end of his four lessons, my pony could jump two feet three inches nicely and I was very pleased.

High Jinks was also behaving well and Jill was confident that he would carry all before him at Stokely. Then, a week before the show, her hopes were shattered—he was lame. No one knew why. Aunt Margaret thought that he should have been jumped in bandages. Jill said that Curtis must have ridden him too fast while at exercise and Curtis that Jill had over-practised him. Barbara and I agreed that it was the fault of Fate.

Altogether Tree Tops was an unpleasant house, full of disagreeable, grumbling people. But I had one consolation; my birthday was the very next day, and I had heard Barbara mention the saddler to Jill the day before, and I felt certain that they must be giving me something for Daybreak.

While I lay in bed that night, I imagined the dining-room table the next morning, loaded with presents and amongst them a bridle, smelling of new leather and with a bit that shone like silver. I did not see a saddle, too, because I thought that no one would give me such an expensive present, but I hoped for some grooming tools, and late into the night I thought about them.

When, at last, the morning came, I dressed with a light heart and whistled as I ran downstairs to the dining-room. I was early; only Susan was there, humming as she laid the table. She stopped when she saw me, and said that breakfast was a long way off yet and that, as the day was cold, she had lit a nice fire in the morning-room. I thanked her and went there and sat down in a chair by the young, smouldering fire. I started to read last week's *Field*, but I was too excited to stay still for long and soon I was wandering round the room picking things up and putting them down again for no particular reason, looking at pictures, looking at books and all the time thinking about my presents, wondering what they were. They could be so many nice things. I remembered that long ago Aunt Margaret had said that I needed a riding coat—perhaps she would give me one to-day. Of course they were rather expensive as presents, but still, one never knew and she was a rich person. Anyway, in case I was given one, I decided that I would like it to be brown and white checked, with two slits behind.

At last the gong rang and, with a view holloa, I dashed down to the dining-room. Aunt Margaret and my cousins were standing by the dresser and they all wished me many happy returns of the day. I thanked them; there were no presents on the table, and I baby-ishly felt disappointed. When we had sat down and started to eat our porridge, Aunt Margaret handed me a flat parcel and said that she hoped I would like it. I thanked her and wondered whether it was a book on horsemanship. With ridiculously excited hands I cut the string and opened the parcel; inside was a flat, leather writing-case.

"I thought that it would help you to keep your letters and envelopes tidy, instead of you always having to search for them. Let me show you the slit for stamps," said Aunt Margaret.

"It's lovely and just what I wanted," I heard my voice lie.

"Here's ours," said Barbara, handing me an almost square parcel.

"Thanks frightfully," I said, and in the excitement of opening it I upset my mug of milk.

"*Augusta!*" said Aunt Margaret.

"Sorry. I'll mop it up," I said, leaping to my feet, and upsetting a pot of sugar.

"Sit down at once," ordered Aunt Margaret, ringing the bell; "you really are the clumsiest child I've ever met."

"*Really,* you *are* queer, Augusta," said Jill.

While Susan mopped up the milk and sugar, I finished opening my parcel; inside were two books. My heart seemed to miss a beat. . . . Perhaps they are about riding, I thought. I looked again and then I was no longer excited. They were school stories; one was called *The Sneak of the Lower Fourth,* the other *The New Girl at St. Martin's.* Both were by the same author and both had twelve shillings and sixpence clearly marked inside. What a lot of money my cousins had wasted on me.

"I hope you like them. When we were twelve we used to love Ann Harding's school stories, didn't we Jill?" said Barbara, in a faintly patronising voice.

"Yes, and those are her two latest," replied Jill.

"Thanks frightfully; they're simply marvellous," I lied.

"Here are three parcels and an envelope which came by post yesterday," said Aunt Margaret.

I took and opened them in silence. I wasn't excited any more; everything seemed flat now.

There was a yellow tie with red people and ponies printed on it, from Penny; an anthology of poetry from an uncle—Mummy's brother—six handkerchiefs from an aunt and a pound from Granny.

"You *are* a lucky little girl," said Aunt Margaret when she saw all these presents.

"That poetry book looks jolly dull," remarked Jill.

"Who gave it to you?" asked Barbara.

"Uncle Marcus," I replied.

"He always was rather a queer man," said Aunt Margaret.

"I think it's a nice book; I like poetry," I said.

106

"Do you? How queer," said Jill.

After breakfast I talked to Daybreak and, although I knew that it was beastly and ungrateful of me, I *did* wish that some one had given me something for him. I hate school stories and I thought of all the nice things my cousins could have bought me for twenty-five shillings—brushes, head-collars, riding-sticks and —oh, so many other horsey objects. Then my thoughts strayed to birthdays at Blenheim Cottage; I remembered that we always had an extra nice breakfast and that, although we were poor, there was always a special treat for the birthday person. Then I realised that my parents had not sent me a present, and I wondered whether they had forgotten me. I expect you will think me beastly and babyish when I tell you that I nearly cried. Everything seemed so horrible and I was very disappointed, because I had hoped for a nice, gay birthday. Now I seemed fated to have a beastly day, and my pony was still without a saddle and a bridle, and I did hate having to borrow my cousins'.

"I do hate this place and every one in it except you," I said, and I buried my face in Daybreak's soft, grey mane. Then Aunt Margaret called my name and I ran indoors. She told me that two parcels and a letter had just come for me, and that she had put them on the hall chest. I thanked her and fetched them. The letter was from my parents; they wished me a happy birthday, and said that they knew that I would like something for my pony as a present. They had, therefore, arranged that I should have five pounds to spend on him; this amount would be given to me by Aunt Margaret as soon as I wanted it. I expect you can guess how pleased I was when I read the letter. I shouted and told my cousins and then, whistling gaily, I opened the two parcels; one was a picture of a horse's head, from my godmother, the other a box of chocolates from Uncle George, who is rich and greedy. I ate three chocolates and then I shouted and asked my cousins whether they would like some. They said, no, eating chocolates so early in the morning was disgusting.

I did not care; now I had five pounds; now I could buy a saddle and bridle. It did not matter that I was disgusting.

CHAPTER EIGHT

WHEN the vet examined High Jinks, he said that he had sprained a tendon and would need at least six weeks' rest, if Jill didn't want him to crack up the first time she had to jump him on hard ground. That cut out all hope of him entering for Stokely or any other show in June, and my aunt and cousins were sunk in gloom. After a lot of discussion they decided that he wouldn't be fit in time for any show before Dilford. "We must be at our very best when we make our first appearance and after six weeks' rest we will need a fortnight to get him fit," said Jill.

However, Sunshine and Sweep were entered for the showing and jumping classes at Stokely, and we all went and missed a Tuesday at school. It poured with rain and we became wet and cold, and my cousins grumbled. Sunshine won the pony showing class, and was awarded yet another cup. Barbara and Sweep were third in the jumping class for children under sixteen years of age. Susan Philips and John Dunlop tied first with their star ponies, Smoke and Paddy. This infuriated Jill. "You wait till Dilford; then you'll

Jumping classes at Stokely.

get the shock of your lives," she threatened, as they received their rosettes.

I remember wondering how she managed to be so confident and sure of herself, but at the time I said nothing, because I began to think of Daybreak and his jumping. A few days ago I had bought him a second-hand saddle with stirrups, leathers and webbing girths, and a stud-billited snaffle bridle. Together, these had cost six pounds fifteen shillings, and with the left-over money I bought a body brush and curry comb. I had discussed Daybreak's complex about brow-bands with the saddler and he advised me to measure and let him know the breadth of my pony's forehead. When I had done this he told me that Daybreak's head was exceptionally broad for his size, and that he would need a full-size brow-band. He sold me one of these with the bridle, which was to fit a pony of fourteen two hands. In this brow-band Daybreak never shook his head, and on the last Saturday before Stokely Show he had cleared a jump of two feet nine inches. Now, as I sat in the car with the rain beating on the windows, the thought of this jump made me feel hopeful. I decided that if I rode properly, Daybreak might complete the children's course on August Bank Holiday.

When Barbara had come out of the ring after receiving her rosette, Aunt Margaret said that we must go home, and my cousins agreed, because they were cold. Two hours later we arrived back at Tree Tops and we all had hot baths, which was very pleasant.

After the Stokely Show the days seemed to drag; then, at the beginning of July, the Dilford Show schedule arrived and we all became very excited. There were four events which especially interested us. They were these:

CLASS 1.—For the Best Pony not exceeding fourteen
11.30   two hands, to be ridden by a child of
a.m.   under fourteen years on the day of the
           show. Judged on conformation and per-
           formance. Entrance fee, 5/-. 1st Prize £3
           and a silver cup presented by Major
           Dewhurst, M.C.; 2nd, £2; 3rd, £1.

CLASS 3.—Children's Jumping. Riders to be under
2.0   sixteen years of age on the day of the show
p.m.   and ponies not exceeding fifteen hands. To
           be judged under B.S.J.A. rules.
           Seven obstacles:
           1. Bush Fence, 3ft. 6in. high.
           2. Stile, 3ft. high.
           3. Gate, 3ft. high.
           4. Parallel Bars, 3ft. 6in. high.
           5. In and Out, 3ft. high.
           6. Wall, 3ft. 6in. high.
           7. Triple Bars, top bar 3ft. high.

Entrance, 5/-. 1st Prize, silver cup value £8; 2nd, £2; 3rd, £1.

CLASS 5.—Bending Race for children under fourteen
4.15   years of age on the day of the show. To be
p.m.   run in heats of four. Entrance fee, 2/6.
         1st Prize, £1; 2nd, 10/-; 3rd, 5/-.

CLASS 7.—Skill and Control Competition for riders
5.15   under sixteen years of age on the day of
p.m.   the show. For the best feat of horseman-
         ship, activity, handiness or skill on the
         part of horse or competitor. No fences or
         equipment supplied by the committee.
         Competitors must bring their own help if
         required. Time limit, 3 minutes. Entrance
         fee, 3/6. 1st Prize, 30/-; 2nd, £1; 3rd, 10/-.

The last of these events was new to the horsey people of Flintshire, but after a lot of discussion Barbara and Jill decided that properly schooled ponies, like Sweep and Sunshine, should be able to win it easily.

"We'll certainly enter and I'll brush up Sunshine's changes of leg and passes a few days before," said Jill.

Later, in the evening, we filled up the entry forms, and my cousins laughed when I entered Daybreak for all the four events that I have mentioned. But Barbara was very obliging and lent me nineteen and sixpence, which I gave to Aunt Margaret, who was writing a cheque to cover all our entrance fees. When she had done this, she told us that, as the days were so long at this time of year, we could all go to bed half an hour later for the next month or two and ride in the evenings, after tea.

We were frightfully pleased, and the very next day we practised our ponies. I offered my cousins a ride on

111

Daybreak and they let curiosity overcome their previous scorn, and accepted. They each rode him for about ten minutes, and all the time I was on tenterhooks and hoping that they would like him. I was doomed to disappointment; Jill said that he didn't understand "direct flexion" and Barbara that he only answered "lateral aids." I said nothing; I had forgotten what "direct flexion" was, anyway. After a few minutes had passed, Barbara said that I could practise Daybreak over their jumps if I liked. I was *awfully* pleased; I felt that this was exactly what he needed. I thanked my cousins and wondered whether it was the excitement of the coming show which had made us all so suddenly agreeable.

High Jinks was still resting, and so Jill wasn't jumping; but Barbara was, and she and Sweep cleared all the jumps at three feet six, with the greatest of ease. It made me feel jealous to watch them, they seemed such a perfect pair, always in time with one another. Somehow, before I jumped Daybreak, I knew that I was going to bungle everything, let him down. I rode him with a heavy heart and made hundreds of mistakes. I didn't send him on fast enough at my cousins' glaring wall; I failed to collect him at all on the approach to the gate; I was left hopelessly behind over the in-and-out, and finally I shortened his stride before the formidable triple bars. All told, we made twelve faults. Jill did not fail to tell me of my atrocious riding, to point out that I had no chance of even completing the course at Dilford. I felt haunted by remorse because Daybreak had tried hard, and I had interfered and let him down. Next time he won't try and I don't blame him, I thought, and hated myself like poison.

When I went to bed I was feeling very disheartened. The thought of the Skill and Control Competition

The very next day we practised our ponies.

worried me, because I could not think of any feat of horsemanship that I was capable of performing. Now that I had jumped so badly, I began to think that I had been conceited to enter. I should only let Daybreak down and make a fool of myself. For a long time I lay awake cursing my rotten riding, my stupidity, my incompetence. Why can't I be like other people? I wondered. Why do I always spoil everything? . . . Then, quite suddenly, I determined to be stupid no longer, to surprise my scornful cousins by some marvellous feat of horsemanship. Now, I stayed awake planning; it was difficult to think of a feat which I could accomplish. I didn't want to perform anything in a saddle and bridle, because I thought that the judges would notice that Daybreak did not flex his jaw properly, and that I was not "gifted" with light hands. I decided to ride in a head-collar and to bring a few circussy tricks into my performance. I knew from experience how easy it is to teach an intelligent pony to shake hands and stand on a tub. At last, somewhere round one o'clock, I drifted into sleep, only to dream of future mistakes and failures.

Next morning I rose early and spent an hour teaching Daybreak to shake hands. He learned quickly and after I had given him another lesson in the evening, he was quite expert. The standing on the tub trick was more difficult, because I had no tub and no money. I searched the garden and all the out-buildings and Jill asked what I was looking for, and I told her to mind her own business. I know this was disagreeable of me, but there is no task I hate more than searching for something which I cannot find. I felt exasperated and irritable, and all the tubs I found were harbouring a cherished flower or self-satisfied shrub, and I could not borrow them.

At last, in utter despair I told Mr. Crisp, the gardener, of how I was hindered from carrying out my ideas; at the same time asking him not to say a word to any one about the things that I meant to teach Daybreak. He seemed flattered at being the only

114

Spent an hour teaching Daybreak to shake hands.

person in the secret, and he went away mysteriously saying that he would see what he could do for me.

Two days later, when Barbara and Jill were out riding, Mr. Crisp told me that he had something to show me. He led the way to the tool shed and there was a stout, black tub. I said, "How marvellous; it's exactly what I wanted. Thanks frightfully." He explained that it was half a tar barrel, and pointed out that he had nailed a piece of sacking on the top, so that my pony's hoofs wouldn't slip. "Thank you; nothing could be better," I told him, and as I gazed upon the tub, I felt pleased.

"Well, you can keep it 'ere at the back of these tools," said Mr. Crisp; "and later on we'll paint it, and don't you let that Curtis catch you practising or 'e will be telling every one—that spiteful 'e is."

"No. I'll get up early and teach Daybreak when no one's about," I assured him.

But, now that I was going to bed later, waking up wasn't so easy. After I had overslept three days running, I asked Betty to call me when she got up, which was six o'clock. She was most obliging and only forgot very occasionally, and then Daybreak missed a lesson, which, I expect was a good thing, otherwise he might have become bored.

Daybreak is very clever and in ten days he had learned to stand on the tub when I waved my hand and said: "Up." He would also jump an old box in a head-collar. Then I decided to teach him to jump with a strap round his neck. This was easy; he went over the box the first time I tried and stopped dead two strides after, and whinnied for the handful of oats I always gave him.

I was very pleased, but I was in rather a quandary, because I couldn't think of a way to get the tub and jump to the show. At last, in despair, I asked Mr. Crisp's advice. He was most agreeable, and said that he thought he could settle the transport for me without much difficulty. Then he suggested that I should use something more spectacular for a jump—a rocking horse or dolls' house would be better, he thought. I said that I would try to think about it and then I thanked him for his trouble and he said that I was welcome.

116

I racked my brain for hours, but I could think of nothing suitable. It was all very well for Mr. Crisp to say a rocking horse or dolls' house, but I had no means of getting them. At Tree Tops unused and unwanted things are got rid of and my cousins are not the sort of people to want rocking horses and dolls' houses; they think that they are too old for such babyish toys. I had no friends either, from whom I could borrow suitable objects.

Eventually, I decided to *make* a spectacular jump, and on Sunday afternoon, while my cousins were reading on the lawn, I cut a grey horse out of a large sheet of asbestos which I found in the store-room. I used a knife and the edges of the horse were slightly ragged when I had finished. He had very poor conformation, too, but I made some charcoal and blackened his mane, tail, eyes and nostrils and then he looked more real. I cut two stakes out of a hedge to lean him against, and I christened him Venture.

At half-past six the next morning, I jumped Venture on Daybreak with a strap round his neck, very successfully. Then I started to teach my pony to follow me when told. This was much easier than I had expected and after three lessons he seemed to understand what I wanted. So by Thursday he knew four tricks—or whatever you like to call them—and I decided to have a dress rehearsal. I borrowed Betty's alarm clock, because of timing it. I pretended that my cousins' "school," which is marked out by white stones, was a ring and I stuck two pitch-forks in the ground to mark the entrance. Then I looked at the clock, gave Daybreak a handful of oats, told him to follow me and walked into the middle of the ring. Here I stopped and we politely shook hands; then, with a wave of my hand, I told him to stand on the tub; this done, I patted him, and said, "Down." He took no notice, but

117

merely whinnied for oats and suggested shaking hands. In the end I had to push Daybreak from the tub and then, when he was on the ground, I gave him the longed-for handful of oats. While he was eating, I scrambled from the tub on to his back, and then we jumped Venture, and cantered out of the ring. I looked at the loudly-ticking alarm clock. We had taken five minutes. I knew that we had wasted three of them at the tub, and I decided to have another rehearsal. This time Daybreak was very good, and we finished in under two minutes.

Later in the week, I taught Daybreak one more trick for the Skill and Control Competition—to canter a figure of eight with a strap round his neck. I did not try to make him change legs in the air, because I knew that I wasn't nearly expert enough; instead we trotted a few steps in the middle and then led off on the other leg; even so, I did not find it easy. Daybreak seemed to edge towards the stable and our figures of eight were more like two oddly-shaped potatoes.

I did not only practise for the Skill and Control Competition; six days a week I rode Daybreak in a saddle and bridle, and twice a week I jumped him round my cousins' course. His jumping seemed to improve quickly and, partly owing to Barbara's and Jill's constant and often cutting criticism, my riding improved, too.

My cousins were also busy practising. High Jinks had started work again during the second week of July, and Jill jumped him four times a week. She schooled Sunshine too; together they accomplished advanced movements like the flying change and full pass, and these never failed to impress me. Whenever I watched them, I realised how much I had to learn, how very, very, little I knew. My supposed "feat of horsemanship" seemed silly—oh, how silly—beside their slick, polished performances. After I had watched these evening practises, I would lie awake far into the night wondering whether Daybreak's and my little act had better not be performed. I would alternately curse myself for a conceited fool and coward. Yet next morning I would rehearse the stupid little act, as usual.

Barbara was schooling two ponies too, because Sandy was "up" and living in the new loose-box, and she was getting him fit for Stephen.

Sometimes we would all practise bending together; this was marvellous fun, only Jill was apt to make excuses when she didn't win, and I was always last, and that spoiled it a little.

Five days before August Bank Holiday, Stephen came home. He had one look at Daybreak, and said: "How I hate greys." I felt disappointed; I had hoped he would like him or, at least, say one nice thing about him.

"Why?" I asked.

"They look like milk-float ponies when they're old and white," he replied; and then he ordered Curtis to saddle Sandy, and went in to change.

A day later Bellaughton broke up and then our show numbers arrived, and I felt terribly excited. All day long, I thought about Dilford, and I became more forgetful and more careless. I was forever losing things now because I was thinking about the jumping or wondering whether Mr. Crisp had settled my transport successfully, or a hundred other things connected with the show. Aunt Margaret told me that I was becoming ruder than ever, and Betty said that I was the dreamiest child that she knew.

My cousins were annoyed with me because I would not tell them what I proposed to do in the Skill and Control Competition. I was very careful about keeping

Venture and the tub well hidden, and so they had no idea at all. They frequently asked whether I had taught Daybreak to change legs or walk on two tracks and when I giggled, and said no, they seemed angry and a little scornful.

Three days before the show, Aunt Margaret took my cousins into Dilford to buy them new shirts. Mr. Crisp and I seized the opportunity to paint the tub. We spent a long time removing all the tar and Mr. Crisp insisted that we should sandpaper it before starting to paint. Every moment I expected the car to turn up the drive, and I worked with frantic haste. Mr. Crisp seemed incredibly slow and, while he sandpapered, he told me how he had arranged for a nice chap, who drove a horse-box, to take the tub and Venture to the showground. The story was long and muddled, and every now and then he paused, so that I should gather the full significance of an especially important sentence. It was maddening and all the time I imagined my cousins scornfully smiling as they looked upon my secret and guessed my stupid little act. "I hope we will finish before they come back," I said.

"Don't you worry, they won't get home for a long time yet," said Mr. Crisp, and he was right. The tub had been drying in the store-house for nearly half an hour when the long-expected car turned up the drive. I was sitting on the lawn, and I felt pleased. Mr. Crisp had painted the tub beautifully in alternate stripes of black and white, so that it would match Venture. He had, also, very kindly given me a black strap, which he said had been lying about his home for ages. It had a shiny, brass buckle and was much smarter than the old belt, that I had always used to put round Daybreak's neck.

Early on Saturday morning Daybreak and I successfully rehearsed the Skill and Control Competition for the last time. Later in the day, we jumped the gate, stile and triple bars at three feet. Daybreak took the lath off the first bar of the triple. Jill said this was because I lengthened his stride too late. I thought that I had pulled at his head on the approach, but I said nothing.

On Saturday afternoon my cousins argued about which of them would win the most prizes at Dilford Show. I cleaned Daybreak's tack and wished that I had a tail bandage and that my saddle was leather-lined instead of serge. I spent ages saddle-soaping, and polishing the bits and stirrups, but when at last I had finished, my tack looked far worse than my cousins', which had been cleaned in a few minutes by Curtis's expert hand.

During tea, Aunt Margaret told me that the cattle transporter had rang up to say that one of his horse-boxes had broken down. He had told her that he could send one horse-box for four ponies only, on August Bank Holiday, instead of the two horse-boxes, which she had ordered.

"I am afraid, Augusta," said Aunt Margaret, "that because Daybreak is the least important and expensive of the ponies, he will have to be the one to be hacked over to Dilford."

"Okay," I said, and I wasn't at all upset, because no one had told me that my pony was meant to go by horse-box, and I had always thought that I was hacking to the show.

"I've had a bright idea," Aunt Margaret went on, "and I've arranged for little Dorothy Shepherd to ride over with you. She's going to meet you outside Dingley Wood at half-past nine, and she will be able to show you the cross-country way to Dilford. That will be fun, won't it?"

121

"Yes, thank you," I said, and I wondered whether Dorothy Shepherd was nice. I did not ask my cousins, because I thought that I had probably met her and forgotten about it. If this was so, I knew that they would be incredulous and scornful.

In the evening I read an article in a horsey magazine on showing ponies. It made everything sound very difficult, and I wondered whether I would fall off again. When I went to bed I was still wondering, but very soon sleep blotted out all forethought. This night I slept a dreamless sleep.

CHAPTER NINE

BETTY wakened me at six o'clock on August Bank Holiday, but, because I had to search for my shorts, I did not reach the field until a quarter-past. Then the sky showed no promise of a fine day; the dark, low clouds even threatened rain, and the very mugginess of the air told the same, dismal story. I had hoped for a brighter morning, but I refused to become cast in gloom.

"Never mind," I said to my pony while I tied him to the gate. "It's early yet." And, whistling, I started grooming. When I had brushed off all the worst mud, I fetched a bucket of soapy water from the kitchen. Mrs. Smith kindly lent me a blue-bag and towel. When I reached the field again, I saw that Daybreak had slipped the halter and was rolling. I cursed and started to climb the gate. I was swinging my leg over the top, when one of my ankles seemed to give way— I suppose this was because I was hurrying—my foot slipped; I lost my balance, let go of the bucket and then, with a soft thud, landed on the muddy ground the other side. I didn't hurt myself; the infuriating part was that I had upset the soapy water; now I should have to go back to the kitchen and fetch some more, and I felt sure that Mrs. Smith and Betty would be very annoyed with me; they had been so nice and obliging before, too. . . . Oh, dear, I thought, why am I so clumsy? Why do I always have to spoil everything? I picked up the bucket and the blue-bag which was covered in mud, and dismally retraced my footsteps to the kitchen. To my surprise, no one was at all disagreeable. Betty laughed when I explained what had happened and Mrs. Smith said that I was to cheer up; by my face any one would think the end of the world had come.

I carried the bucket of new soapy water to the field without mishap and I caught Daybreak easily. I spilled a great deal of the water into my shoes while washing his tail, and lost the blue-bag twice and the towel once. I had just finished, when Curtis arrived and fed the other ponies. I asked him the time, and he said that it was seven o'clock. With a start, I realised that I must get a move on if I wanted Daybreak plaited and ready by a quarter-past nine. He was dirty again now, after his roll and would need grooming with a dandy brush, all over again.

I brushed twice as hard this time, but the mud was wet and clung to his coat like clay. I had made up my mind to leave the grooming and start the plaiting, when the breakfast bell rang. Then I left the field and tore down the garden path towards the house. In my haste, I did not look where I was going, and I tripped over a stray stone and fell. Luckily, I didn't seem hurt and I leaped to my feet and ran on. When I reached the dining-room, I felt blood trickling down my legs and hoped that no one would see it. I hurried to my

Start the plaiting.

chair, but as I was preparing to sit down Aunt Margaret noticed.

"What *have* you done now, Augusta? Your knees are covered in blood," she said.

"Only fallen down," I replied.

"Really!" said Jill. "What a babyish thing to do."

"You are queer; fancy falling down," said Barbara. Aunt Margaret said: "Go up to the bathroom and wash those knees, at once; then put on some Iodine and sticking plaster and lint. You'll find plenty in the medicine chest in my bedroom. Hurry up or your breakfast will be cold."

"But they're only grazed and they don't hurt," I said, not wanting to waste time.

"Do as you are told and don't argue," ordered Aunt Margaret.

"Okay," I said.

When I arrived back in the dining-room, having dealt with my silly knees, the others were eating toast. I glanced at the grandfather clock that stands in a corner of the room. The time was five minutes past eight.

"Oh, dear! I must hurry," I said.

"I hope Curtis has given Sandy the extra two pounds of oats," said Stephen.

"I told him to give High Jinks two three-pound feeds; one at six o'clock, the other at nine-thirty," said Jill.

"Need I have any toast?" I asked.

"Yes, you must; you won't be having anything else until one o'clock," Aunt Margaret told me.

"I hope he's put Sweep's mane into seven small plaits this time—that is what I ordered," said Barbara.

"Are you feeling nervous, Gussy?" asked Stephen.

"No, I'm in a hurry," I replied, stuffing a piece of toast into my mouth without butter or marmalade.

"May I go now?" I said, leaping to my feet.

"When you have finished your milk and rolled up your napkin," replied Aunt Margaret.

When I had done as I was told, I persuaded Aunt Margaret to lend me a needle and a reel of grey thread. Then carrying these I ran back to the field. Daybreak was still tied to the gate and he whinnied when he saw me. I brushed his mane and then searched the tack-room for a mane comb. I looked in vain. Curtis, also plaiting, was using the only one. I cursed and fetched my hair comb from my dressing-table. With the help of this I started plaiting. I found, at once, that it was not so easy as I had imagined. Daybreak *would* fidget and hundreds of times I dropped or lost the needle and scissors, and pricked my clumsy fingers. When I had sewn and un-picked the second plait three times, I began to lose my temper. I started to shout at Daybreak whenever he moved, and the angrier I became and the louder I shouted, the more he moved and the more I pricked my fingers. It *was* exasperating and every moment the time was later and the children's jumping class nearer. I thought of how late I was going to be, and of Dorothy Shepherd waiting outside Dingley Wood. I pictured her small with short, fair hair and an anxious face.

"For goodness' sake, stand still, Daybreak," I shouted, and then I hit him.

"Never lose your temper with a pony," said a calm voice directly behind me.

I looked round. There was Jill, clean, smart and unruffled in her best riding clothes, coming to see whether the groom was preparing her three-figure ponies to her satisfaction. For a moment I felt hot with fury. "Shut up, you selfish prig," I shouted. Then I patted Daybreak, because I was sorry that I had hit him; and I noticed that it was beginning to drizzle with rain.

"What a temper to be in on August Bank Holiday," said Jill, and she passed on towards the stable.

"Isn't she a beast?" I said to Daybreak, and suddenly I wasn't in a temper any more. I felt quite calm in spite of knowing that I wouldn't be ready by a quarter-past nine. I even whistled the "Skye Boat Song."

I had finished the last plait—the forelock—and was standing back, hoping to be able to admire it, when Aunt Margaret called to me from the passage window.

Shouting: "Coming," I ran indoors and found that the time was five minutes to nine.

"It's time you changed, and mind you put my needle and thread back in my work-basket," said Aunt Margaret from the top of the stairs.

"Okay," I said, and I ran to the field again and fetched them, and shoved them into the work-basket. Then I tore to the bathroom and washed. It was not until I reached my bedroom that I found a piece of red cotton was following me, and then I was in too much of a hurry to do more than silently decide that Fate was against me. I hurried frightfully, as I changed, and the cotton was maddening; when I drew on my jodhs it clutched the clip at the bottom of their legs; when I pinned my new tie it tangled round the pin, and when I brushed my hair it meandered amongst the bristles of my brush. I broke it three times, but it would not leave me. I was on the point of screaming with exasperation, when, to make matters worse, Aunt Margaret called my name.

"What is it?" I shouted.

"You naughty little girl, how dare you spread red cotton round my house?" she called from the bathroom.

"Sorry, sorry, sorry," I shouted, and now I was frantic with haste because it was five past nine and I could not find my shoes.

I searched my bedroom in vain; I dashed to the nursery and looked there and then I tore downstairs to the dining-room. All this time the red cotton followed.

"Betty, Betty. Please have you seen my shoes?" I shouted.

The kitchen door opened. "They are in their place," said Betty.

"Where is their place?" I said. I always left them at the foot of my bed.

127

"Under the dressing-table. You ought to know that," she replied, shutting the door.

"I've looked there, and they aren't," I said, but I ran back to my bedroom just in case I had made a mistake.

Of course, Betty was right; they *were* under my dressing-table, looking very smug, too; as though they were telling me that I ought to have started by searching properly because, "lazy people take the most pains."

I roughly forced my feet into the irritating shoes and then tore downstairs again. At the bottom I trod on one of the untied laces and fell over.

"Oh, dear, everything seems against me," I said, as I picked myself up.

Then Aunt Margaret appeared through the drawing-room door. "Augusta," she said, "what has come over you? You do nothing but fall down. Are you ill?"

"No. I'm in a hurry and everything possible is hindering me. In a minute I shall go mad," I said.

"Don't talk such nonsense; it's your own fault you are late. You shouldn't waste so much time trying to be funny and spreading cotton around. This is not Blenheim Cottage, you know. Your mother may have stood your jokes, but let me tell you, I'm *not* going to. You just collect all that cotton and put it back in my work-basket this very minute."

As Aunt Margaret finished speaking I felt myself grow hot with anger. The very suggestion that I should think it funny to be followed and hindered at every corner by some beastly red cotton infuriated me. As if I wanted to waste time playing practical jokes on a gymkhana morning.

I wanted to be dignified. I said: "I am sorry; you have made a mistake; I am not trying to be funny. I would scorn to make such a prep-school joke even in this—this horrid, proper house." Then for the first time I noticed the cotton was tangled round my shirt sleeve's button. With a cry of joy, I broke it and ran from the house.

Daybreak seemed pleased to see me and he stood very still while I put on his tack. It was raining hard now and the clouds were low and grey. My shirt was already slightly wet and was beginning to stick to my body. I felt that my luck was out to-day. I mounted and then I saw Stephen. "My! Gussy," he said, "you've put that bridle together all wrong. Look, the snaffle's back to front."

"Gosh, I shall go stark, staring mad in a minute," I said.

I mounted and then I saw Stephen.

E

"All right, don't panic. I'll put it right for you in half a tick," said Stephen.

"Thank you," I said, and I remembered the black strap which was to go round Daybreak's neck. "I've just got to go indoors for something," I added, dismounting and tearing to the house.

In the hall I met Barbara. She handed me my tweed coat, with the two silver buttons missing, and told me that Aunt Margaret said I was to wear it. Then she laughed and said that she had persuaded Mummy not to make me clear up the red cotton to-day, and that I had better hurry, because it was nearly half-past nine. I thanked her and, although I knew I would look incorrect in the coat, I put it on, because it's no good arguing with grow-ups and, anyway, I was afraid that if I didn't Aunt Margaret might make me tidy up the cotton, after all. When I had fetched the strap I found Stephen holding Daybreak saddled and bridled in the front drive; I thanked him and mounted. "His plaits are not exactly up to Olympia standard," he remarked, and I said:

"No, they aren't, are they?" And I rode away down the drive.

"Good luck," shouted Betty from an upstairs window.

"Thank you," I shouted back.

When I reached Dingley Wood, which is roughly a mile and a half from Tree Tops, there was no sign of Dorothy Shepherd. I waited in the entrance of it; and the rain splashed through the mass of greenery above my head and made clear, clean, little puddles on the pebbly ground in front of me. I shouted, "Hoy," several times, but my voice mocked and came back to me in an empty echo. Daybreak soon became impatient; he refused to stand still any longer and pawed the ground, and occasionally neighed. . . . What can have happened? I wondered. And I guessed that Dorothy Shepherd must have tired of waiting for me. "Come on, Daybreak," I said, and I rode back along the lane and took the main Dilford road. Here, the world seemed a noisy place. Hooting cars filled with gay, smiling families, gaudy, back-firing coaches packed with whooping, waving people, goggled men on spitting motor-cycles, quieter folk on push-bikes, horse-boxes, which made my heart beat faster, earnest hikers, giggling pedestrians, slow caravans; all passed me in an endless stream. They splashed Daybreak's legs with water and I thanked heaven that he was quiet in traffic.

I could not hurry; the road was too slippery, and we were forced to walk. Every moment I expected Aunt Margaret's car to glide softly by, but as time went on I realised that she must have taken the quieter road to Dilford. I should have chosen it too, I knew that now. I would be late and it was my own fault; I had been in too much of a hurry to stop and think, and now I was going to pay for it. As I rode along the broad black road, I felt very glad that Aunt Margaret was not here to tell me that I had only got what I deserved. I remembered that I had been making silly mistakes all morning. Fate is against me, I thought, and then quite suddenly I realised that I had forgotten to bring my number. "Oh, gosh!" I said aloud. "I shan't be able to enter." I expected to be overcome by a wave of disappointment, but instead, I thought: Perhaps it will be a good thing. I would have only fallen off in the showing class, and we would have refused three times at the bush in the jumping and forgotten everything in the Skill and Control Competition. Much better not enter, not make a fool of myself.

"Gosh! I'm a coward," I said to Daybreak, and I

131

noticed that one of his plaits was coming unsewn. Then I thought of Mummy and of how much she despised people who were afraid of making fools of themselves. I remembered her telling me it was a sign of narrow-mindedness, and I felt annoyed with myself; then I thought of Mr. Crisp, Mrs. Smith and Betty all expecting to see me compete and I wanted to be in time. "Come on, walk up, Daybreak," I said, and I squeezed with each of my calves in turn.

When we reached the suburbs of Dilford, I saw myself in the shop windows, and I must say, I looked awful. My hair was wet and hanging lank and straight like rats' tails; my face seemed incredibly dirty and my tweed coat looked ten years old, and very dingy. Daybreak looked nice, but two of his plaits were now unsewn and mud still clung in brown patches to his grey coat.

Here, in the suburbs, were notices and arrows pointing the way to the show and many people were hurrying and catching buses going in that direction. I felt very excited. I wanted to enter now. A tall, dark woman passed me wearing a black coat and boots, and perfectly-fitting peach breeches; she was riding a chestnut hack. They both looked smart and the chestnut's mane was beautifully plaited, and I felt very conscious of my own slap-dash appearance.

A little later a clock chimed the half-hour, and I supposed it to be half-past ten; but in case I was wrong I asked an old woman the time. To my horror she replied: "Half-past eleven."

"Oh, gosh! Thank you," I said and, in spite of the road still being slippery, I urged Daybreak into a trot. We clattered through the crowded streets and passed the smart woman on the chestnut hack—she looked disapproving—and reached the suburbs on the other side of the town, in a few minutes—or so it seemed.

Now I hoped that I was near the showground, but it was not so; before me stretched a long, straight road bordered by villas with hideous gables and glaring windows, with neat gardens and bright little gates. I saw no sign of a show, no flags, no horse-boxes, nothing but the long, long road, the satisfied villas and above, the gloomy grey sky.

I heard the neighing and clapping.

On and on we went, sometimes walking, mostly trotting, and I always scanning the horizon. It was like a horrible dream, the sort which make you wake with a flat, empty feeling. Nobody had told me that the showground was so far the other side of Dilford, and I pinched myself and made sure I was not sleeping.

At last I saw flags and bunting, and then I heard the neighing and clapping, which accompanies horse shows. My heart leaped with joy. I was in time for the Skill and Control Competition, and the jumping and they mattered more to me than any other events. I felt like shouting hooray, but I kept my mouth shut, because there were many people about and I did not want to be thought "queer."

A few minutes later I rode through the Competitors' Entrance, at the same time remembering, with a wave of disappointment, that I had no number. I scanned the showground for my cousins, but in vain. Tents, horse-boxes, cars and one solid mass of people hampered my view. How large the ground is too, I thought, and I felt that I must be dirtier, more untidy, more incompetent than any one else there.

"Hullo, what happened to you?" said a voice behind me.

I turned round; it was Mr. Crisp. "Have I missed the showing class?" I asked unnecessarily.

"Yes, it's just finishing," he answered.

"Do you know where the Collecting Ring is, please?" I asked.

"I'll show you," he said.

Mr. Crisp talked while he wended his way through the crowd of horses and people. I paid little attention, because I was thinking how smart every one looked compared with Daybreak and me. Then I heard him say, "I'm sorry, but there it is."

"There what is?" I said.

"The horse what you made."

"Oh, did he get here safely? Thank you so much."

"No, that's just what I'm telling you. Some one let a horse step on him and bust him up."

"Oh, gosh! Everything's going wrong. What am I to do?"

"Perhaps we can find something what'll do instead; I'll 'ave a try, anyway," said Mr. Crisp.

I thanked him, and then I saw Stephen, looking very smart in his checked coat and black bowler. "Come on, Gussy," he shouted. "You've missed seeing Jill carry off her usual first in the showing class."

"I say, hadn't you entered for it?" said Barbara.

"Yes," I answered.

"What a swizz," said Stephen. "Still, you wouldn't have won anything."

"I've forgotten to bring my number, anyway," I said, dismounting.

Barbara smiled. "Typical of you, Augusta," she said.

I felt very downcast, and I knew that she was right. "But what shall I do?" I asked.

"That's all right, I'll get you a new one," she replied, and rode away towards the secretary's tent on the neatly-plaited Sweep.

It had stopped raining so I took off my coat and Stephen pointed out Aunt Margaret's car, and I led Daybreak to it and chucked my coat in the back. Then, still feeling dirty and untidy, I returned to the Collecting Ring. I found Jill, smiling happily, surrounded by admiring people. "Hullo, Augusta," she said. "I've done it again."

Suddenly I felt very disagreeable. "You mean Sunshine has *done it again*," I said.

As I spoke, the crowd of admirers seemed to turn like one and fix their eyes upon me. "Coo, look at that grey pony, ain't he dirty," said a boy.

"Doesn't look as though 'e's been brushed for months," commented one of his companions.

I turned and led Daybreak away. "Will all competitors for class two come into the Collecting Ring," blared the loudspeaker.

"Augusta, what has happened to Dorothy?" called Aunt Margaret.

135

"I must put High Jinks over a practice jump before lunch," said Jill.

CHAPTER TEN

I DID not feel downcast or disagreeable as I waited in the Collecting Ring at ten minutes to two. I only felt slightly sick, and that was through excitement and, in a way, quite a pleasant feeling. I had unplaited Daybreak's mane and brushed all the mud from his coat, and he had cleared the practice jump of three feet six a few minutes ago. Now the sun was shining and competitors were taking off their coats, so I looked all right in my shirt. Everything seemed to be taking a turn for the better and this made me more hopeful.

My cousins and Susan Phillips and John Dunlop were in the Collecting Ring too. Jill was telling every one about High Jinks. "You should see him—five feet is a mere nothing; but then he *is* a properly-trained, show jumper."

No one was taking much notice of her; they were too busy thinking about *their* ponies. John Dunlop kept apart from his fellow competitors. His checked cap was crammed down on his head; his black gaiters and breeches were splashed with a little mud. His blue shirt and braces looked clean but old. He seemed calm and confident as he walked Paddy round, occasionally nodding to some one in the crowd.

Susan Phillips sat very still, looking pale and cold. Her long yellow plaits dangled down her back and clashed with her brighter-yellow shirt; her small hands nervously fiddled with Smoke's plaited mane. She looked more like a miserable child of nine ready to burst into tears at any moment, than a famous child-rider. A small, wiry woman with hard features, and pale hair enclosed in a hair-net was giving her last instructions. "Drive her fast at the wall," she said; "don't let her stick her toes in. Remember, use your spurs as you reach the wings."

"Yes, Mummy," whispered Susan.

Mr. Crisp ducked under the Collecting Ring rope, and walked to me. "Would a rocking-horse do instead?" he asked quietly.

"Yes, beautifully. Thanks frightfully. Where did you get it?" I said.

"I've got a niece what lives in Dilford; it belongs to 'er, and will be on the showground round about four —a chap in a lorry is bringing it."

"You are clever; how nice of your niece to lend it to me. Thanks awfully."

"She's a nice kid. Well, best of luck. I must be getting along now—see you later," said Mr. Crisp, and then he ducked back under the rope and was lost in the crowd.

"Will all competitors for class three come into the Collecting Ring," blared the loudspeaker.

I looked around me and started to count the waiting riders.

Jill was talking to a dark girl in a crash cap on a brown blood pony.

"In fact, five pounds less than Sunshine," she said.

"Yes, and he was cheap at that," said the dark girl.

Barbara was watching Curtis, while he polished Sweep's already shining bits. She looked well dressed in her fawn breeches, brown boots and checked coat, and her hair seemed neat underneath her correctly fitting, black bowler.

Beside me, Stephen was talking to Aunt Margaret, who was sensibly dressed in a tweed coat and skirt.

"It's the limit to ride a ripping pony like Paddy in braces," he said in what he seemed to think was a quiet voice.

"What a fright little Susan Phillips looks too, with those long plaits," said Aunt Margaret. "Why doesn't her mother have her hair bobbed? It would look much neater."

"That pony over there looks as though it came out of a milk-float. I bet it can't jump a thing," said Stephen, waving scornfully at a skewbald cob.

Then I moved away from Aunt Margaret and Stephen, because I did not want to be connected with them and their ceaseless criticism.

I finished counting; there were twenty-five competitors. Eighteen of them were entered in the programme, so seven were late entries. How smart and professional they seemed to me. None of the ponies looked as though he would refuse three times in front of the first jump. . . . I shall be the only person to be disqualified, I thought.

The judges walked into the sunlit ring, carrying shooting sticks and judging cards; two were wearing riding clothes, one a suit.

The Collecting Ring Steward walked to the dark girl on the blood pony. "You're first," he said.

"Oh, golly!" she said. I was surprised; I had expected her to be calm and superior.

"Bad luck," said the boy on the dock-tailed skewbald cob, which Stephen despised.

"Number three hundred," blared the loudspeaker.

The dark girl cantered her pony down to the bottom of the ring and turned him, and rode at the bush fence. He cleared it with ease, and the stile, and the gate. I wished that I could ride as well as the dark girl; she looked nice in her navy-blue coat, and she sat beautifully. Before jumping the parallel bars, competitors had to pass the ring entrance and here the blood pony broke into a trot. I could see the dark girl squeezing with her calves, trying to make him canter.

"Poor Jane. Vanity is up to his tricks again," said the boy on the skewbald cob.

"He needs re-schooling," said Jill.

The brown, blood pony laid back his fine ears, swished his pulled tail and refused the parallel bars three times. "To think that pony cost a hundred and forty-five pounds. Some people *do* get done," said Jill.

The dark girl patted Vanity and cantered out of the ring, looking as smart and elegant as ever.

"Bad luck," called the boy on the skewbald.

"He always does it now," shouted the girl.

"Number three hundred was disqualified. Number three hundred and one is now coming into the ring," blared the loudspeaker.

"Good luck, son," said a small man wearing a homburg hat, as John Dunlop rode through the entrance, looking calm and determined. Paddy walked with short, springy steps; his docked tail carried high, his ears pricked. He soon reached the far end of the ring.

"Now we will see something worth seeing," said some one watching from the ringside.

John cantered his pony in a small circle, before approaching the bush fence.

"He thinks it helps to balance his pony," explained Jill.

Then, crouching far forward in the saddle, John made Paddy canter very, very slowly, until he reached the wings of the jump. Here he thrust his hands forward; his pony dashed and with a whisk of his fat quarters cleared the bush fence.

"They are *sure* to win," said the boy on the skewbald, dismally.

139

"If Susan Phillips doesn't," added the dark girl.

"Don't you be so sure," said Jill.

A minute or two later, John cantered through the exit amid a storm of applause.

"That was a clear round," blared the loudspeaker.

"I told you so," said the boy on the skewbald.

"I shall have to jump off against him," said Jill. "Curtis, are you sure that High Jinks's bandages are tight enough and is his hood adjusted properly?"

Susan Phillips's number was three hundred and two and when, still seeming pale and nervous, she rode into the ring, I heard her mother say: "Remember now, spurs at wall." Susan held the single curb rein tightly, and trotted down the ring with her toes pointing towards the ground. She looked more feeble than the dark girl, and Smoke seemed lazy compared with Vanity. It struck me as fantastic that this nondescript pair should have won so many prizes. Smoke trotted towards each jump with her ears laid back. Then, three strides away, they would go forward, her stride would lengthen and a few feet in front of it she would take off. Seven times I expected her to make a mistake, but she cleared all the jumps and, like Paddy, left the ring amid a storm of applause.

The next competitor was Stephen; he cantered Sandy to the bottom of the ring and approached all the jumps at a fair hunting pace. The boy on the skewbald said that it looked as though Stephen would make another clear round, but the dark girl said that they wouldn't and she was right. Sandy knocked a brick off the wall and the top bar of the triple with his front feet.

"Eight faults," shouted Stephen, as he galloped through the exit.

At the same moment, Barbara walked Sweep through the entrance, looking indifferent and slightly

140

bored. She cantered slowly towards the bush fence. She did not saw at her pony's mouth like John, but sat very still; the reins were loose. Sweep went with his ears back, as though he had jumped too often, was even bored by it. When they reached the wings, Barbara kicked; he cantered a little faster, took off and cleared the bush fence by the fraction of an inch.

"*Anyhow, she'll* do a clear round; *she* always does," said the boy on the skewbald.

This time he was right. Barbara and Sweep cleared each jump in the same dull style.

"Well done," said Aunt Margaret, as they left the ring.

"Now it's me," said Jill.

When High Jinks trotted down the ring he looked flashier and more dashing than any of the other ponies. He pranced and sidled and snorted, and his tail and head were carried high. His tasteful grey bandages hid his white socks and the black hood made him seem mysterious—as though he had something "up his sleeve." Jill smiled happily, and I knew that she was thinking that her great chance had come at last.

The small man in the homburg hat turned to John Dunlop. "It looks as though Jill Fielding has got something hot there," he said.

Aunt Margaret was talking to one of the judge's wives, close to the Collecting Ring. "I paid a good price for him, and I expect to see my daughter win to-day," she said.

I patted Daybreak and remembered that my number was three hundred and six. I had not been thinking of myself lately. I had been too busy looking at, and listening to, my fellow-competitors.

Now I looked at Jill again; she was at the bottom of the ring turning High Jinks. He seemed very "showy"

Something like the cowboys on the films.

and I wished that Daybreak pranced in the same, impressive manner.

Then, quite suddenly, an amazing thing happened High Jinks reared, came down to earth and reared again. Jill sat perfectly with the reins loose and her body forward. A silence descended upon the crowd at the ringside, all eyes were fixed on the pony and rider —here at last was excitement for the onlookers— something like the cowboys on the films.

An age seemed to pass before High Jinks stood on all four feet again; then, with a snort that cut the silence like a knife, he threw down his head and galloped across the ring and out by the exit.

"Take him back, Jill," shouted Stephen.

"My pet, what are you doing?" called Aunt Margaret.

"Whoa. Whoa, High Jinks," shouted Jill.

"Three hundred and five is disqualified," blared the loudspeaker.

"You're next," the Collecting Ring Steward told me.

"Oh, gosh!" I said. "Come on, Daybreak."

We walked into the ring. All round us seemed faces —faces cramming and pushing by the ropes; faces gazing from cars; faces watching from horses—looking at Daybreak, looking at me. I thought, we've got to surprise those faces; we've got to do well; we've got to win. I squeezed Daybreak's sides; he trotted; we reached the bottom of the long ring.

"Good luck," said Betty's voice.

The bush fence loomed ahead, black and formidable; the faces faded. "Come on, Daybreak," I said. He cantered. Three strides from the take-off, I squeezed with my calves; he cantered faster and then we were over the bush. . . . This is lovely, I thought. Now the stile was in front of me; it looked small and tempting. Again I pushed Daybreak faster a little way before, and again he jumped clear. It was the same over the gate, and we passed the entrance amid an outbreak of claps. I patted Daybreak, and we turned the corner and he pricked his ears, and flew the parallel bars, and in-and-out. Then before us was the grey and white wall, looking small, but very stout. Daybreak's ears went back; he hesitated and his stride shortened. . . . We mustn't refuse, I thought. I squeezed and then I kicked; he pricked his ears and we were between the wings, and then we were over the wall. I looked back—no brick had fallen. . . . Only one more. We *must* clear it, I thought. We turned the corner; Daybreak was going faster now, and the triple was coming nearer every moment. Three bars, all to be cleared.

"Steady, steady," I said, and I tried to collect my pony. The next moment we were almost on top of the bars; then we were in mid-air—and over—we hit nothing.

"Clever, clever, Daybreak," I said, and we left the ring our ears filled with the sound of clapping.

Outside the exit, I fed Daybreak on all the oats I could find in my pockets.

"Jolly good," congratulated the dark girl.

"You'll win," said the boy on the skewbald.

"That's a grand pony," remarked Mrs. Phillips.

"A clear round," blared the loudspeaker.

I felt very pleased; more pleased than I had ever felt in my life. I've done it, I thought, I've surprised everyone. "You clever fellow," I said to Daybreak.

Some one was jumping in the ring, but I did not watch. He came out and the onlookers clapped half-heartedly, so I guessed he had made several faults, and thought of Jill. I felt sorry for her, because I knew how beastly it is to be disqualified especially in a horse show, and I thought it must be even more horrible when you had expected to win.

"You'll have to jump off," the boy on the skewbald interrupted my musings.

"I hope you win. John Dunlop and Susan Phillips need to lose. I'm tired of seeing them carry off all the prizes," said the dark girl.

"Thank you," I said; "but I know I won't. My clear round was only a fluke. I shall ride badly and let Daybreak down next time."

"Nonsense; you rode beautifully. I wish I could ride like you," said the dark girl.

I felt my face turning red and I looked the other way; I did not want anybody to see that I was blushing.

The boy on the skewbald went into the ring. "I know I shall have three refusals," he said. He rode very badly; he kicked, and flapped his legs and his cob refused three times in front of the parallel bars.

"Bad luck, Martin," shouted the dark girl, when he cantered through the exit with a downcast face.

"Augusta," called Aunt Margaret, "could you go and fetch Lord Langley? He's in the only Rolls-Royce in the seven and sixpenny car park, and I want him to come and have a look at High Jinks."

"Okay," I said, knowing that there were about eight competitors waiting to go, before the jump off.

"I'll hold your pony. It will be easier to get there on foot," said the dark girl.

"Thanks awfully," I said, handing her the reins.

I wended my way through the crowd, whistling the "Isle of Capri" and no longer feeling dirty. I found the Rolls-Royce easily; inside was sitting a dark man with disagreeable features. I hesitated; he turned round and saw me.

"Good-morning—I mean good-afternoon," I said. "Are you Lord Langley?"

"Yes, I am," he replied, and his tone was cold.

I said: "Oh! Well, Mrs. Fielding" (he scowled at the sound of the name) "asked me to ask you whether you could possibly come and look at her pony—he's in the Collecting Ring."

Lord Langley frowned; then he said, "Will you tell Mrs. Fielding with my compliments that I am not (a) a veterinary surgeon, (b) a horse dealer, (c) a professional adviser; and also I propose to stay here and watch the rest of the show from my car."

"Okay," I said. "She won't be pleased."

"I don't mean her to be," he said, and then he looked at the ring again. I walked slowly to the Collecting Ring and found Aunt Margaret and my three cousins close to the exit.

"He won't come," I said.

"Nonsense," said Aunt Margaret.

145

"No, it's true," I said, and I repeated Lord Langley's message.

"Good gracious, Augusta; you don't seem able to open your mouth without irritating somebody. You *must* have been rude to Lord Langley. He is so fond of Jill, too," said Aunt Margaret.

"I'm sorry, but I wasn't a bit rude," I said.

"Three hundred and one, three hundred and two, three hundred and three and three hundred and six have to jump off," blared the loudspeaker.

"Come on, Augusta," said Barbara. I fetched Daybreak from the dark girl and mounted, and rode into the Collecting Ring with Barbara and Sweep.

The stewards were altering the jumps; they widened the distance between the parallel bars, raised the in-and-out, put another row of bricks on the wall and heightened the triple bars.

"Now, take her slowly at the in-and-out, and don't forget to push her at the wall and triple," Mrs. Phillips advised her daughter.

"I'm hot," I said, and deep down in the pit of my stomach I felt hollow. . . . If only we could do another clear round, I thought.

We had only the last four jumps to compete over this time. John Dunlop cantered a small circle before approaching the parallel bars. Paddy was excited, and sweating, and fighting for his head. "He's in fine mettle," said the man in the homburg hat to Aunt Margaret; she did not reply—she was looking at Barbara and Sweep.

John and Paddy took the parallel bars fast and cleared them easily. I felt certain that they would not make any mistakes, but my heart pounded wildly and my eyes were glued to the famous pair. On they went, cantering dead slow and then something went wrong; they seemed to increase their speed too late; there was

146

Several people shouted, "Well done, John."

a rapping noise and the first bar of the in-and-out fell to the ground.

"Sheer bad luck," muttered the man in the homburg hat.

"Hooray," said the dark girl in a tactlessly loud voice.

I hoped that I wasn't smiling or showing how

pleased I felt. Barbara's face seemed expressionless, as though she didn't care whether she won or lost.

John and Paddy cleared the wall and triple bars, and as they left the ring several people shouted, "Well done, John."

"That was two faults," said the dark girl.

Susan Phillips rode in next; an anxious frown creased her pale face and she still clasped the single rein tightly. She used her spurs on the approach of the parallel bars, but Smoke took it too slowly and hit the second one with her front feet. Afterwards she went faster and they cleared the in-and-out beautifully and the wall by some miracle, but Susan did not push the unwilling Smoke hard enough when they reached the triple bars, and she knocked off a lath. My heart gave an unsporting leap of joy; I had some hope, now.

"One hundred and four," announced the loud-speaker.

Barbara trotted into the ring on Sweep, and cleared the parallel bar and in-and-out, by the fraction of an inch. I hoped she would beat John Dunlop, but as she approached the wall, I saw Sweep's ears lie flatter than usual and I noticed that he was slowing up. Barbara kicked—one, two, three—at the last kick he was supposed to take off, but instead he refused. Barbara hit him with her stick and he swished his beautifully pulled tail. Then she rode him back a little way and tried again, but again he refused.

"She's only got one more try," said Mrs. Phillips, and by her voice I knew that she was glad.

"Hit him," shouted Stephen, from the ring side.

Barbara turned Sweep and rode towards the wall for the last time. When she reached the wings, she changed the reins into one hand and used her stick with the other. Sweep swished his tail; his ears shot back; he refused. Barbara hit him twice and then I squeezed Daybreak and we trotted into the ring. This time I did not notice the faces; my eyes were on the parallel bars; they looked low, but broad and I was determined to ride faster than Susan Phillips. Three strides from the take off I squeezed, expecting Daybreak to hurry more. I was not ready when he refused and I nearly shot over his head; only the sight of the muddy ground and the thought of making four faults stopped me. With a mighty effort, I managed to slide back down his neck into the saddle.

The crowd laughed and clapped, and I was determined not to let Daybreak refuse again. The second time we approached the parallel bars I kicked him three times instead of squeezing and he flew them. Then he cleared the in-and-out and wall and, last of all, the triple bars. The crowd cheered and clapped, and Daybreak almost galloped out of the ring. When I had made him slow down to a walk, I started to dismount, but I was interrupted by the loudspeaker calling my number. I hastily rode back and led the way to the judges; my heart pounded against my ribs like a ton of bricks and now, I noticed the ring of faces, but this time I did not care. I had won the jumping and that was all that mattered to me.

The judge in the suit handed me a red rosette and a silver cup. "Well done. That is a splendid pony," he said. I thanked him and put the rosette in my mouth and waited for the others. Then, when they were ready, Daybreak and I led the way round the ring at a canter. The crowd clapped again and at the far end, Mrs. Smith and Betty shouted: "Well done." I felt myself growing red and I knew I was smiling, in spite of having to hold the rosette. When we cantered through the exit, the dark girl shouted, hooray, and the boy on the skewbald, jolly good, and I pinched myself to make sure that I was not dreaming. It all seemed too good to be true. As soon as I had slowed Daybreak into a walk, I dismounted and tied the rosette on to his brow-band. Barbara was tying her white one on to Sweep's bridle.

"Well done, Augusta," she said, and she smiled, not scornfully, but in a sporting way.

CHAPTER ELEVEN

AT twenty minutes past five o'clock, I was again waiting in the Collecting Ring. This time, I was holding Daybreak in a halter, and he was wearing the black strap round his neck, because the next event was the Skill and Control Competition. Mr. Crisp was at the ring side with the rocking horse and tub; I could see him out of the corner of my eye, and I was very excited. The dark girl and the boy on the skewbald wanted to know what I was meaning to do. Every few minutes the boy would say, "Please *do* tell us," and then, when I refused, the dark girl, "You are a beast."

All the waiting people seemed very agreeable, now, and several patted Daybreak and asked questions about him. Stephen was pleased because he had won the bending race. He talked about school and football to a boy named David, who had been second on a pony called Tomtit.

I had been last in my heat in the bending and Jill told me that I hadn't used my legs enough as I turned the end post. Mr. Crisp said that I had been asleep at the start and Betty, that I had been dreaming as usual.

Now, while I waited, I resolved to keep very wide awake. I told myself that I must be really brisk in the next event, because of the time limit. One thing worried me—the rocking horse. Would Daybreak jump it in the ring? Earlier in the afternoon he had jumped it behind a tent. Then he had been wearing a saddle and bridle and he had hesitated and only just cleared it. What would he do in a strap in the middle of a large ring? I asked myself this question again and again, but of course I could only wait and find out the answer.

At last the suspense was ended. The Collecting Ring steward told me that I was the first competitor and was to go into the ring. I waved to Mr. Crisp and the loudspeaker announced my number. With a fast-beating heart, I told Daybreak to follow me and walked through the entrance. I heard the dark girl's voice say, "Go on, Daybreak." I looked round; my pony was following. I plunged my hands deep in my pockets and did not look behind me again until I reached Mr. Crisp with the tub. He put it down, and I stopped and shook hands with Daybreak. Then, with a wave of my hand, I told him to stand on the tub; he hesitated and for an awful moment I thought he was going to gallop out of the ring. Then, with slow dignity, he stepped upon it. The crowd laughed and clapped and I began to enjoy myself. I managed to make Daybreak step off the tub easily, and then I jumped on to his warm, grey back. We cantered the figure of eight, and it wasn't quite the right shape, because Daybreak would edge towards the other ponies. Then I looked for the rocking horse. For a moment I couldn't see it and I wondered whether it had met with the same fate as poor Venture, but on running my eye round the ring, I spied it in the exit with Mr. Crisp and Betty standing on each side, so that we couldn't go through without jumping it. I was glad that they had thought of this, because Daybreak was becoming very excited

151

and, in a strap, I had no real control. We approached the exit at an extended canter and when Daybreak saw the rocking horse he pricked his ears and went faster. I sat very still until a few strides away, when I squeezed his sides and grabbed the mane. I was only just in time; he took off far earlier than I had expected and if I hadn't been holding on to something, I think I would have fallen off.

We were followed by a multitude of claps, as we cantered on across the showground. Daybreak seemed pleased with himself and some moments passed before I managed to slow him down to a trot. and then a walk, I jumped from his back while he was walking. and put a hand on his nose and made him stop, and fed him with oats.

Then a strangely familiar voice said, "Bless me if it's not Jackson's pony." I looked round; there behind me was the man who had advised me not to buy Daybreak.

"Yes, I bought him for fifteen pounds—I mean guineas—at Dilford Market," I said.

"Well, you've done marvels, miss; marvels," said the man, staring at Daybreak with incredulous eyes.

"Why?" I asked.

"Mr. Jackson couldn't do a thing with him, that he couldn't, and that's a fact," the man went on, "and he knows a thing or two. You wouldn't find *him* selling a pony at Dilford unless there was something very wrong with it."

"Please tell me, what was wrong with this pony?" I asked.

"Well, it was like this——" The man leaned against a tent pole, wiped his face and started to tell me Daybreak's history.

I am not going to repeat his exact words to you. partly because I can't remember them, and partly be-

Jumping the Rocking-Horse.

cause he told the story in a very long-winded and incoherent way.

This is my version of it:

For the first four years of his life, Daybreak lived in the farm where he was born, in the midst of the Berkshire downs; then he was broken by the son of the farmer, who owned him. He apparently behaved well, and a year later he was advertised for sale as a thoroughbred, New Forest cross, which was quiet with hounds and a promising jumper. Mr. Jackson was looking for a pony of that size at this time and, when he saw the advertisement, he stepped into his car and drove to the farm and saw Daybreak. The farmer's son had recently broken a leg tobogganing—so the farmer said—and Mr. Jackson had to trust his word and only see Daybreak led in hand. In spite of this, he was very struck by him and eventually bought him for thirty pounds, which he thought cheap. When Daybreak arrived at his new home, Mr. Jackson tried him and was appalled to find that he had a frightful head-shaking habit. During the next fortnight Mr Jackson rode him in twelve different bits and five different saddles, but none made any difference; the shaking went on. At last, in despair, he called in a local vet, who examined Daybreak carefully. He watched him ridden, drinking, eating and tested his wind, and at the end was at a loss to know what to say. Eventually he told Mr. Jackson to turn Daybreak out in a field and rest him for a fortnight, and said that he would come and see him again at the end of this time.

Mr. Jackson did as he was told, but when the vet came again, Daybreak shook his head in the same way as before. The vet thought for a long time and asked hundreds of questions, before giving his verdict, which was—the beginning of a tumour on the brain. He advised Mr. Jackson to sell the pony at once and then he left with a frown creasing his forehead, because he was not certain that his verdict was right. Mr. Jackson was an honest man, and he now thought Daybreak dangerous, and so he decided that he must be sold in the market without a warranty. Then he would be either bought by gipsies or somebody who fancied himself as a breaker in. . . . As you know he was bought by neither, and I must say I still think I was very, very lucky to get him.

When I had thanked the man for telling me Daybreak's history, I hurried to the Collecting Ring with a fast-beating heart. I wanted to tell my cousins why my pony had been sold at the market, and to hear what they thought of his performance in the Skill and Control Competition. Jill was in the big ring, cantering perfectly shaped figures of eight. She and Sunshine looked the perfect pair, so neat, so correct and yet so picturesque. I decided that they were sure to win, and I noticed that my shirt was covered in Daybreak's slobber and my hair straggling over my eyes.

Then, on my left, I heard Mrs. Phillips talking. I tried not to listen, but her voice was loud and sentences seemed to float my way. "Yes, that's Jill Fielding," she said. "She wins a lot with that pony, but she's not putting up a good show now. She's got the pony behind the bit and it's only changing legs in front and she hasn't noticed. It's shocking how many best rider prizes she wins. . . ." Mrs. Phillips's voice dropped and I moved and heard no more. Then suddenly it filled my ears again, loud and clear. ". . . buying that pony from Tom Smithers, I thought every one knew that it always does that in the ring now. Why, Ann Wake would have kept it if it hadn't turned vicious like that—it reared right up with her, you know, at the Padley Show and broke her back. . . ."

At this point, Mrs. Phillips lowered her voice again, because Jill was cantering out of the ring accompanied by a few half-hearted claps.

The dark girl, who was on foot now, walked to me. "That was worse than yours," she said.

"Oh, no," I said. "Mine were only badly done tricks and hers was horsemanship."

Barbara rode into the ring and she too, cantered figures of eight and rode full and half passes and serpentines. They seemed very complicated and clever to me, and I was even more certain that I had no chance of winning another rosette. While Barbara and Sweep performed, the dark girl told me about the other competitors, who had been competing when I was listening to Daybreak's history; she said that not one of them had ridden so well as me. Of course I didn't believe her, but her words brought hope dancing in front of my eyes again, and I could hardly stop myself from skipping with excitement.

After Barbara, a small boy on a Shetland pony walked into the ring and wandered aimlessly around for a few minutes, before coming out again. I felt sorry for him, because he reminded me of my performances on Dominoe, and he obviously couldn't make his pony do what he wanted.

"I think you will win," the boy on the skewbald told me.

"Sssh," said the dark girl, "he was the last competitor."

"Seven hundred and one, seven hundred, seven hundred and nine and seven hundred and five, please come into the ring for your prizes," blared the loud-speaker.

"Go on, you're second," said the dark girl.

"Gosh!" I said, as I followed a fair-haired boy on

156

a heavenly chestnut mare, into the ring. Barbara was behind me and beyond her was a girl, whom I hadn't noticed before. Her hair was in small, dark plaits and she rode a bay horse. We all lined up in front of the judges and I remember that I smiled and then hoped I didn't look conceited. The fair-haired boy was given a red rosette, Barbara a yellow, the girl with plaits a white, and I a blue. The judges only said well done, to all of us this time; I expect they were tired of thinking of complimentary remarks or perhaps they thought we didn't deserve one each. We all cantered round the ring with the rosettes in our mouths and the fair boy went so slowly that I had difficulty in stopping Daybreak from trotting. The circle of faces smiled and everybody seemed to be clapping, and I felt very happy. When I had cantered out of the ring, I found Mr. Crisp and Betty and thanked them for their help. Then I tied the blue rosette beside the red on Daybreak's brow-band, and I must say he did look nice; the colours of the two rosettes suited him perfectly.

A few minutes later Barbara and Stephen came and congratulated me. They were awfully agreeable and not scornful or patronising Barbara said that my riding had improved beyond recognition, and Stephen that the strap riding had been ripping. Both of them told me that I couldn't be expected to beat the fair-haired boy in the Skill and Control Competition, because he was riding a highly schooled show hack, which had won dressage tests. I said that I was sure he was a better rider than me anyway, and that my win was only a fluke. Then Barbara said that I was ridiculous and Stephen that I was queer—not to be pleased when I won prizes. I said that I *was* pleased, terribly pleased, and then we saw Aunt Margaret beckoning. We led our ponies to her, and she said that it was time to start for home. Barbara asked whether we could stay and watch the Open Jumping, but she said, no.

Stephen said, "What a swizz," and Jill asked

Clever Daybreak.

whether he *never* thought of his pony; surely he realised Sandy would be happier in his stable than standing in a stuffy horse-box, she added. Then she went on, "And as for you, Augusta, unless you start for home soon, Daybreak won't get back until after dark, and I'm sure he wants a long night's rest after his tiring day."

"Prig," I said in a cheerful voice, and then I started whistling.

"Augusta!" said Aunt Margaret. "How dare you call Jill names. I can see your wins have gone to your head already. Jill is quite right, you must start for home now and think of your pony before yourself."

"For once," added Jill.

"Shut up, Jill, and mind your own business," said Stephen. "Augusta is right you *are* a prig and, what's more you are conceited and think that you're a marvellous horsewoman—really you can't ride for nuts."

"Stephen!" said Aunt Margaret.

"I'm going home now," I said, and mounted and rode from the showground, and left the excitement, and clapping and quarrelling behind me.

I took the quieter road to Fledgewood, this time, and I met little traffic. I remembered how I had ridden Daybreak here in a halter a long time ago, when we hardly knew one another. I felt very happy; so many of my dreams had come true, so much had happened since then.

Occasionally a car whizzed by us, with gay, holiday-makers inside, but often the curling road was almost silent and then the birds held the air and filled it with the gay, trivial songs of summer. I remembered how, on a sunny day weeks before, I had wished for a farm-house with a white front door, and a spaniel with flopping ears and a few ponies. Now I did not want any pony, but good, clever Daybreak, who had cost fifteen guineas from the worst market for miles around and won two rosettes at his first show.

Slowly, while we walked, my thoughts turned to future shows and were lost in a maze of victory; and

159

all the time the long day was ending. The birds voices ceased. Wrapped in red and gold, the sun drifted in to sleep, behind the darkening beechwoods. The air grew chill and the sky of a deeper, greyer hue. Slowly, carefully the land slept.

When we turned on the Fledgewood road, I heard a train hooting a long, long way away; it broke the soft stillness of the evening. Later, I saw the lights of Tree Tops; they lay golden across the narrow road, like broad bands.

"Clever Daybreak," I said, and then I started to whistle.